Dedicated to dreame

for those who ar

and have the co

Davide R. Battaglia

SOMEWHERE I BELONG

Photograph by Minjung Kim, edited by Marco Battaglia.
Content reviewed and edited by Sarah Chidgey, with the collaboration of Jill Rippingale and Darren Van Der Merwe.
ISBN: 978-0-578-79301-6
Original title: *Il Posto Più Bello Del Mondo*
Sponsored and distributed by VistaLounge News LTD & www.vistalounge.net

Turn off your mind and let your thoughts go.

Rebel against a life that does not feel like yours and to which you do not belong.

Take a risk. Take the first step. It does not matter where or how, but do it.

Travel. See the world in all its glory.

Consciously choose your sense of direction. If you do not know how, seek it, at any time, in every corner of your soul.

Fall and hurt yourself. Get up. Repeat the process.

Rest, listen to yourself and heal your wounds: it's not true that "it's nothing".

Ignore the "unapologetic judges" and understand them: they have already surrendered to a life of pain, compromise, fictitious certainties and that's all they have; without that illusion of "right and normal", they would be lost and terrified.

Surrender to the bloody fear of uncertainty; open-up to the new and the unknown.

Continue on the road you felt you wanted to travel.

Rediscover your joy, the joy that has been dulled by a sense of duty and the feeling that the weight of the world is on your shoulders: life is not just pain and sweat.

***LIVE** fully! Every sunset, every goal, every friendship, every lover, every sip of beer. And also, every defeat, every disappointment, every failure. It is all part of the game and it is okay. You were not born to be a mere spectator of your existence and it makes no sense to watch life run away from you. You are the protagonist, the choreographer, the actor, and the creator: you live following the plot of the most beautiful show you can ever think up or imagine. Get up from that seat, take in the scenery and start living the true story of your life.*

1.

"WHAT AN ASS!"

After a seven-hour flight and barely one hour of sleep, I was awakened by the colourful remark of a very refined local passenger behind me, who reached the highest peak of his regal elegance, turning with a two-fingered whistle to a flight attendant who had just bent down to pick up a pillow.

I was still not quite sure what I was doing sitting on that plane, however, my desire to change my life once again had been greater than any rational plan, seizing the first opportunity that had knocked on my door.

After seven years of living in London and a few months between Singapore and Bali, without thinking twice, I had embarked on yet another new adventure on the other side of the world, chasing a stranger, who I had barely passed by at a jazz bar.

"Attention please, passengers are advised that flight SC 489 will be landing at your destination in fifteen minutes. Please return to your seats and fasten your seatbelts."

The surrounding white expanse of clouds suddenly faded away, leaving room for the deep, varied blue colour of the Indian Ocean and the thousands of colours of the city below, offering a breath-taking view of the land of kangaroos, which became closer and closer as we descended.

A few moments later, I heard a deaf thud and here I am.

"SC Airlines welcomes you to Sydney."

A new chapter in my life had just begun which, although I was still unaware, would soon change my life forever.

But let's take a step back. Or rather, ten.

My name is Oliver, a guy who grew up in the last golden years of Italy, the '90s. Golden years that vanished as soon as I finished high school: I found myself in front of a world and a society that were in total chaos, a country that was changing but did not accept change, a wealth that was disappearing without the willingness to realise it. So, I found myself at eighteen years old with a dishrag of a diploma in my hand, in a new city and no idea how to even begin making my way in this life.

I had grown up in the province of Turin, in the middle of the mountains, in a quiet, cold and rather arid emotional reality. Life was pretty much set, as well as the people. The important thing was not to complain, because at the end of the day, it wasn't so bad; I couldn't find real meaning in that kind of life. From a young age, I never felt completely comfortable in that kind of reality, however, I never paid too much attention to it. On the contrary, many times I thought I was the one who was mistaken, and I tried to be more like the others, without ever getting much satisfaction out of it.

I lived in a really remote village, located in the middle of the woods, where not even public transport passed through. My first real opportunity to start any sort of social life was not until I reached fourteen, when my father bought me a moped: a legendary 20-year-old Honda Bali with 20,000 miles of eggplant colour, then converted it into a tacky electric blue with fluorescent green wheels. It (almost) never broke down, but it was disarmingly slow. One night I remember running into a huge boar with its litter afterwards. I swerved and accelerated to avoid it, but the road was all uphill; I still remember the sight of the beast in the small mirror chasing me, at a quicker pace than my poor Honda Bali, with its fangs out and a pissed off look, while I had already started to recite my last prayers.

Fortunately, the rabid animal stopped halfway, perhaps out of pity for my moped.

I lived with my father in a modest cottage on top of a hill, cheap rent, given the total isolation of the place.

He was not very present, he worked almost every day and when he came back, he was often upset and in a bad mood, so I tried to keep the conversation to a minimum. He tried to be a good father, in his own way, but without conviction. He had been working for a famous chocolate cookie factory for over thirty years, and was a man now resigned to a life of pain and without any particular joy or satisfaction, especially since he had lost my mother.

I remembered her as a beautiful woman, strong and charming. She had very long black hair down to her shoulders, a stern but sweet face and a very slender physique, as far as I could remember.

She left when I was only seven years old and I never knew the precise reason.

I still remember that day, one late November evening in 1994. My mother held me tightly to her in a long embrace, her eyes full of tears, whispering in my ear: "I'm sorry. I am so sorry. Always remember that mum loves you so much and will always love you. Never lose hope."

She stood up, wiping her make-up with a handkerchief and, taking her things quickly, leaving the door behind her. That was the last time I saw her.

I had always wondered what the real reason was, sometimes blaming myself, thinking I had done something wrong. I missed her embrace and her presence every day. Then, as I grew up, I had learned to live with her absence, without ever accepting it inside of me. I had asked my father more than once, the reason for that gesture, where she had gone and why I couldn't see her, but every time I touched on the subject, he would stiffen up and change the subject quickly. The last time we discussed it, I was eighteen years old, I had just finished high school and we were coming back from my graduation ceremony. We started to discuss it in the car and a furious argument broke out.

I hadn't seen my mother in eleven years and demanded to know how things were, at least if she was well and alive. After twenty minutes of heated conversation, the only thing he could come up with was: "Forget it. You would not understand. In life, all chapters have a beginning and an end and this one was closed a long time ago. It's just you and me that matters, we're not doing so badly after all".

When he spoke, I could feel all the pain he was feeling inside, despite his calm and rigid appearance. It must have been really something big and I'm sure that, in his own way, he was trying to protect me and prevent me from getting hurt. I looked at him with a smile and hugged him. He remained rigid. His eyes were shiny and he saw that I noticed them.

"What the fuck are you smiling at, you moron?! They even gave you a diploma!! Come inside and let's open this bottle, it's been waiting five years for you."

My grandfather had bottled a special wine for the day I got my diploma and there was even one for my university graduation too, which is still there on the shelf.

"Congratulations Oliver, welcome to the shitty world of adulthood! Cheers!"

"Thanks dad, it's nice to have someone so positive and enthusiastic near you, you are a real joy!"

“Well, You’re too big for fairy-tales. You have to start opening your eyes. At least we have our health…!”

After a good half hour of cynicism and negativity, he took the opportunity to tell me that his company was relocating him to Rome, he told me that he would be leaving in a couple of weeks. Without too much enthusiasm nor too many regrets, I decided to follow him.

I had always possessed a strong sense of responsibility and propensity for duty and I had matured earlier than I should have, leaving no room for the bullshit that teens usually get up to. It was the fault of the village, its sober atmosphere, without ever being excessive, and maybe, even a little bit, in part due to my family situation. So I imagined, back then, that Rome would have been a good chance to live a late adolescence, the one I had not enjoyed in high school.

There in the Turin valley, I used to go out with some classmates from time to time, but I never really had fun. I was quite a nice guy, but also a bit shy and clumsy: tall, brown and intense eyes, with hair that naturally stuck out, always straight and messed up, similar to a Japanese manga character; I didn't put very much effort into styling it, I woke up with it already like that in the morning. My old maths teacher once told me that the hair reflected the personality of the individual and, in my case, she was probably on point.

The fact is that, although I was one of only eight boys in the high school, I didn't get much done, some flirting at parties organised by my school mates, though nothing more.

During a summer's evening, a friend of mine invited me for a night-out in his town, located half an hour away from my house, or forty minutes on my old Honda Bali. I remember that there was an event, something called "No-Tav Festival", against the upcoming high-speed train, with concerts of (very) amateur groups, rivers of alcohol and a large attendance of people who came with the sole intention of getting wasted. I remember it like my first hangover: after finishing a whole bottle of limoncello, I turned towards the stage, shouting at the top of my lungs about how I was in favour of the high-speed train, because in my imagination I could have arrived earlier at school in the morning. Obviously, in that moment, I had no idea what it was (and that the project consisted of the Turin-Lyon route instead of a regional train).

I risked being lynched, but my friend Alex managed to limit the damage, convincing them that I was a poor drunken asshole with no knowledge and dragged me away quickly.

That same evening, I met Luana, a neighbour of his who we met on the way back, while I was still in a total state of alcoholic delirium. She was a very simple girl, but intelligent, with whom it was pleasant to talk to; dressed in a very flashy way, with purple lipstick, high heels and miniskirt, she certainly attracted attention.

People knew her as bad news, especially in that small reality with an extremely narrow and provincial mentality, because of her frequent visits to youth clubs and the hustle and bustle of various boys she was seen around with, but to me she seemed like an interesting person.

We exchanged phone numbers and, the next evening, we found ourselves sitting on a bench in the woods.

She became my first girlfriend, we kept each other company during the last two years of high school, only to lose touch with each other after graduation. That was the highest emotional peak of my adolescence.

2.

In Rome things went differently. In the early days I was in a state of shock, due to the total change from a small, tediously tidy, and quiet place to a big city, constantly messed up and disorganised. Moreover, having just finished high school, I didn't know anyone at all.

I spent the first few months in solitude, I missed my certainties, the tranquillity of the village and even those few asshole friends I had left up there. Then, as time went by, I managed to open up. It's really true what they say, when we find ourselves outside our comfort zone, the truest part of ourselves emerges and we are finally ready to give up our fears, our mental patterns and habits, we are able to welcome the new in more easily. And I must say that, for a while, I had a lot of fun.

One evening I was walking alone in Trastevere, trying to enjoy it, a bit melancholically, that typical Roman midsummer evening. The street was all lit up with lights that ran along the river, surrounded by majestic trees and with a lively and festive atmosphere. I sat on the little wall, opened a bottle of beer that I had bought at a nearby bar. I felt at peace with the world. For a few minutes I left aside all the anxieties and thoughts that had accompanied me up to that moment and began to enjoy the view, sipping my Peroni. I remembered an article about the law of attraction, which I had read some time ago, which, at first, I did not really believe: when you put positive vibes into the universe, it sends them back to you in some form.

That evening I met Gian and Daniel; they came to scrounge a cigarette off me and we started talking about many things, and discovered that we all lived in the same area.

They soon became my best friends. We went out practically every night and a true and sincere friendship developed between us. We never did anything special, most of the time we just sat on a bench drinking beer, smoking and shooting the breeze, just for the pleasure of being together. Then, around two in the morning, if we still had not had enough, we would go to Daniel's house to play the PlayStation until the early morning.

His father was not at all pleased about it. He was a strange man, in his sixties, originally and proudly from Venice, he too ended up in Rome god knows how. We always tried not to wake him up, but inevitably after the first wrong goal in FIFA, someone would raise their voice; in a few seconds, there he was in the living room in his underwear and tank top, swearing wildly at his son, in his very strong Venetian accent, which always resulted in loud laughter from everyone, leading him to get pissed off and blaspheme even more, slamming the doors and screaming at the top of his lungs in the middle of the night.

I wasn't proud of it, but I laughed too, they were scenes worthy of the best comedy show.

One night, at the pivotal moment of the situation, the poor man tripped over the cat, which, taken by surprise, scratched him, making him stumble against the glass table, which in turn made him fall against the wall cabinet of the ceramics, where his precious Venetian masks hung, which came down, shattering into a thousand pieces along with everything else, in a perfect Mr Bean like scene that woke up the whole landing. We had tears in our eyes and our stomachs were hurting from how much we were laughing, at which he got seriously angry and kicked us out of the house, yelling the most incomprehensible insults and ordering us never to be seen again. It was all worth it though; in fact, it was one of the best moments ever.

Apart from my new friendships, I also started to meet many girls in Rome. I was twenty years old; I was in top physical condition and I had become quite an extrovert a great combination for attracting female attention.

Actually, I have never been a true womaniser, one of those people that collects notches on their belt. I always liked to get to know women in depth and I still believe that each one has something to give and teach. However, if after a certain number of dates, I felt simply that there wasn't enough to warrant continuing the relationship, I would move on, to avoid wasting time with one another.

In any case, I felt that my glorious second adolescence, after a year of drinking and fucking around, had almost come to an end. The evenings began to become all the same and I fell into apathy. Gian and Daniel were taking other paths, which I didn't feel like following. Although I felt I deserved that little break, as a sort of compensation for my high school years, which I never lived to the fullest, it was time to get back on track.

I enrolled in university, in the Faculty of Communication Sciences. I had always been told that I was good at writing, the only advice I had ever received so far, so I chose that option, in the faint hope of becoming part of a newspaper in an imagined utopian future. I went there for about two years without ever really feeling comfortable. I hated the way the system was structured, it got on my nerves. Professors without passion, without soul or decent temperament, who pontificating a lot of nonsense, protectors of a system already obsolete twenty years ago. Everything was in total disarray; exams postponed without notice, classes that demanded obligatory attendance with five-hour gaps in between, subjects included in the program without any logic. I wasn't even doing too badly, even if I refused to buy or photocopy the huge books we were supposed to study, I always passed the exams anyway, showing up in the morning and listening to those who were reviewing the subject.

I remember once when my friend Elisa, a southern girl that I had met at the course, had studied the entire program per top to bottom for three months, while I barely knew the title or the subject of the exam, showing up there still half-drunk after a night spent drinking at the home of a classmate of mine. She gave me a couple of quick tips in just 20 minutes. I passed the exam with excellence, she failed. She didn't speak to me for weeks, but later we became very good friends.

One day, during a very heavy lesson of "communication languages", after the umpteenth and repetitive obviousness spewed by the professor, something snapped in my head. I got up and put on my coat. The professor stopped talking and stared at me.

"Are you going somewhere? Have you already learned everything?"

"No, the problem is just this, that in the two years here I haven't learned anything. And I had enough of these platitudes." I replied amidst general perplexity.

The professor stared at me almost in shock.

"Do as you like, everyone in life eventually finds themselves having to deal with the results of their own choices”.

"It is perhaps the most sensible thing I have heard you say today, and I thank you for that last pearl of wisdom".

I turned my back and left.

Thinking back on it today, I could perhaps have left with less fuss, but what I can say is that it was probably the best choice.

3.

After I left the university and never went back, I found a part-time job as a handyman in a Kazakh association in Italy, where I practically sat there for four hours reading the newspaper while they were doing Kazakh lessons and opening the door when someone came in. I had the keys to the office, which was in a fantastic location, because it was located in the centre, near Via dei Condotti, where more than once I had invited girls on the sly. Especially Mara. She was a tiny petite woman, very smiley, with a very nice face and the biggest breasts I had ever seen.

We got to know each other in a rather unusual way. We were on the subway and I noticed her staring at me. At first, I pretended like it was nothing. When we got to the next stop, she got off with me and asked me to give her a kiss, without even talking to me before. None of my friends could believe it, but that's exactly what happened. From then on, we started going out a lot, but basically, we always ended up just in bed. Or rather, everywhere except in bed.

It certainly wasn't a great job and the contract was only for three months, but then again, that's the only thing I could expect to get at that time and with only a shred of diploma in my hand, while I was trying to decide what to do with my life. It also allowed me to work four days a week, just to have some money in my pocket to buy clothes, cigarettes and to get drunk with friends; the rent was paid, and food was not lacking. The only problem was that this association, located, as I said, in the centre of the city, was more than an hour away from my home and, not having a car, I had to rely on public transport, which, in Rome, is incredibly unreliable.

After my last weekly shift, I grabbed my coat and went to the station.

The usual train at 17:30, which was delayed until 18:40, that day in December was busier than usual. A flock of commuters were trying to make their way through the crowd in that cramped wagon, some with their first round of Christmas presents, some with their briefcases, after another monotonous day of work. I found myself crushed in a corner near the door. To my left, a bearded, tall, burly man grabbed the handrail, placing his armpit a few millimetres from my face. An intense and nauseating smell penetrated my nostrils and, for a few seconds, I struggled to hold down the vomit, managing to find a bit of a relief a few centimetres further away.

After twenty-five minutes of agony, I finally arrived at the Piramide stop, where another amusing hour on the bus would be waiting for me, not counting the waiting time, on which I was betting with my "companions of adventure", who kept increasing in number as the minutes went by, leading me to wonder how such a concentration of human beings could ever enter a single vehicle. After a good half hour of waiting, finally the bus arrived from the end of the street. A moment of general joy and liberation and as the wild race to a seat began, then the one for the place to stand

and, finally, the search for a few inches of remaining space that, finally, would have allowed us to go home.

The bus pulled over at the next stop, where four people got off and nine people got on, crushing us even more like canned sardines. Among them was an elderly gentleman trying to get on. He was quite obese, glassy eyes, sloppy clothing and his breath reeked of alcohol. He walked with difficulty and was blabbering on; he didn't look homeless, but you could tell he wasn't in good shape. A lady offered him her place. He sat down and, as he was sitting, I don't know how deliberate it was, but he let out roaringly loud fart, which silenced everyone for a few seconds.

A series of varied blasphemies echoed throughout the bus, coming from a group of kids at the back, which got worse due to the rancid and pungent smell that, in a few moments, had enveloped the entire bus.

Two stops were still left to go, but I had had enough for the day, so I decided to get off early.

Finally, some peace. The temperature was a bit harsh, but I had warmed up in that bus sauna and I needed some air. I used to observe the other people around me a lot, especially to understand what gave them the strength to accept all this, every day and at all hours. Above all I saw a lot of discontent and resignation on the dissatisfied faces of the people and I wondered if there was a way to change things and if so, who was I compared to them who had accepted, with dignity, for the most part, that this was normal and in the end it was fine.

I began to walk along the side streets on the outskirts of Rome. I didn't want to be disturbed by anyone in those twenty minutes that separated me from home, even though, perhaps, at the same time, I needed someone to hug me and say, “It's okay, it's just a moment, it will pass soon.”

A moment that had been going on for three years now and seemed never ending, while I felt less and less motivated every day. I couldn't see any way out of my situation, but life always surprises you when you least expect it. The wind of change was just around the corner and was about to unleash a storm, which would change my stupid, monotonous and senseless routine forever.

4.

I have always been an impatient person who can barely stand still for long. The monotony of my life in Rome was depriving me of any stimulus. It was not so bad for me, but not so good either. It was a very stale, superficial and empty period. I had no idea what I wanted to do "when I grew up" and I lived from day-to-day, at a very slow pace. I would drink a couple of beers and walk alone until three in the morning to fall asleep. I felt as if I was wasting my life, continuing to wonder if existence was really limited to that.

One day, plagued by total boredom, I found myself scrolling through my cell phone's address book and decided to contact Elisa, my former university friend, for a coffee.

Another winter had passed, and the first spring sun was shining high in the sky. It was nice to see her again after a long time. She had become even prettier. She had a white dress with a flower pattern that accentuated her curves, olive skin and highlights in her thick hair, which brightened up her face. She was about to graduate and pursue her dream of becoming a web designer for a newspaper. She wasn't much of a writer, but with the computer she could create graphically extraordinary works, which compensated for her literary deficiencies. I noticed that she had developed some nervous tics since the last time, like continuous shivers every time I said something.

"Have you started to take drugs or are you annoyed by my presence?!"

When I asked my question, her twitch from annoyance became even more pronounced and she poured hot coffee on my pants, burning my crotch area.

"Oh gosh forgive me!! I’ve become overwhelmed since preparing my thesis, I'm exhausted".

She took off my pants to try to remove the coffee stain and got a cream to relieve the burning. After a few seconds of embarrassment, she began spreading the cream on my crotch area, which was getting me excited. She noticed and, after a few seconds, her hand slowly slid up and started jerking me off. I took her in my arms and slammed her on the table, I lifted her dress and opened her legs; then I moved her panties and pushed myself inside her, and she started moaning with pleasure, holding me tightly against herself. It was very intense and spontaneous. When we finished, Elisa had no more tics.

After a few seconds of embarrassment, we got dressed and smoked a cigarette together, before continuing to discuss our uncertain futures and the good old days, as if nothing had happened.

"I really have to go now. It was really nice to see you again!"

"Wait, Oliver!", she stopped me.

"I wanted to tell you that tomorrow at three o'clock there is the national writing competition in English. They are holding it nearby. I remember you were doing quite well in both English and writing!"

"Thank you, but I think that chapter is closed for me now".

"Are you sure? For the top ten, there is an internship at the Times in London for a month... Think of the possibilities that would open up for us!"

Those last words made me flinch. After all, what did I have to lose, apart from a few hours, which I would have otherwise spent with a couple of beers. In addition, my contract with the Kazakh association had expired and I think they had also clocked on to my extra work activities, so it was not renewed. I'd been trying to find another job for months, never getting an answer, and my savings were starting to dwindle. This might be a good opportunity to put myself out there in a different way and finally get out of this monotony.

"Wow sounds cool. All right, you've convinced me! I'll see you tomorrow then, I'll pick you up at two so we can go together."

"Perfect. But no coffee tomorrow!"

We both burst out laughing and after a sincere hug, we went our separate ways.

On the way home, I thought about the contest and what it could mean. I could leave, leave that apathetic life and pursue my old dream, now stored in the most remote drawer of my unconscious. I did some online research on the event, which I was able to subscribe to in time, a few minutes before the deadline and could tell it was important. There were people coming from all over Italy to have that unique chance, which probably meant they had been preparing for months, people with much better English and cultural background than me. However, I decided that I had to try; in the worst-case scenario, I was sure I could convince Elisa to go for another coffee.

5.

The next day I went to pick up Elisa, on time, from under her house and we walked to the venue where the competition was being held. She was very elegant; she was wearing a dark grey suit and an unbuttoned blouse, hinting at her ample bosom which was enticing me. I was wearing black pants, a white shirt and a grey jacket. My father once told me that if you have to go into battle, of any kind, you must always look impeccable, as it gives you more confidence. I had never fully believed it, but that day I decided to follow his advice, perhaps even a little bit out of superstition.

We arrived at the front door.

"Are you ready?" I asked her. She was very tense. She did not answer, closed her eyes and began to breathe deeply and noisily. Her tics had returned.

"Do you want a coffee?!"

"You are an idiot! Come on, let's go, it's late."

The room was full of people, mostly in their thirties and there was a surreal silence. Most of them had anxiety printed on their faces. All of a sudden, we met Alberto, a dear former classmate of ours with whom we used to spend our university afternoons.

"Hey! Long-time no see! You here too?! I am happy to see you again!", he exclaimed; "Can you stick around after you have finished? I would like to catch up!"

I answered him that I would wait for him in front of the entrance. Elisa barely smiled and nodded her head; she was becoming more and more nervous.

I was calm. I have always been in such circumstances; I had an enviable cold-bloodedness. As an alternative profession, I could certainly have considered a job in the bomb squad, cutting the wires to defuse them.

We went to fill out the form and then sat down together. An

extremely serious and intimidating guy, wearing a pair of extremely thick glasses, read us the instructions of the article we had to compose.

"Very well, now turn the paper over and get started. You have four hours from now."

One last look at Elisa and then I started to tidy up my ideas. I was fine, I had a goal. When I have a goal in front of me, I get excited, I always manage to give the best of myself. I finished ten minutes before the time was up, I handed in my paper and went to smoke a cigarette, waiting for the other two to come out. After few minutes, I finally saw them come out and joined them.

"How did it go guys?"

"Quite well I think, then we'll see", said Alberto, with his typical tranquillity.

"I don't want to talk about it", answered Elisa. "Let's go for a *Spritz*".

Regardless of how it went, I was already happy to be able to spend an evening in their company, especially seeing

Alberto again. He was a sort of good, gentle giant; six and a half feet tall and weighing almost twenty stone, very friendly and pleasant to meet, who always put people in a good mood. A simple and genuine person, with a lot of talent when it came to writing. When we worked for a few months for the university newspaper, he was my most bitter "rival", our articles were always the most interesting and appreciated.

He told us that his father's butcher's shop was not doing well and he had started working as an assistant chef at a Mexican restaurant to continue paying for his studies, but he had just been fired because the chef caught him sneaking appetisers into the refrigerator.

"They were feeding me half a burrito or a plate of pasta and beans, how did they expect me to work on an empty stomach?!"

Elisa and I burst out laughing, especially because he was really convinced that he hadn't done anything wrong. In the meantime, he had vacuumed up practically the entire table of canapés included in the aperitif, getting disapproving looks from the waiters and the owner.

At the end of the evening, one Spritz became ten and I had to take Elisa home on my shoulders, so we exchanged numbers and said our goodbyes, while he was intent on swallowing the last few slices of bread and wasabi snacks.

Fifteen days later, I was sitting on Elisa's couch, drinking another “coffee”, when we received an email with the results of the contest. I had almost forgotten about it, as I did not have high expectations and I was convinced that those who knew someone in the judging committee would have won, no matter what. Elisa opened the Excel document with the rankings and looked in amazement on her cell phone, squinting her eyes.

"Well? Who won? Did you...?!"

She looked at me, accentuating a melancholic smile, I could see that she was disappointed but at the same time excited:

"Third place: a certain Eleonora Pavini; second place...Oliver Milani!!"

"Me? Are you serious?!"

"I'm not joking! Read it!"

"I can't believe it! I never would have expected it! And who is the first one?" I went to read at the top of the document:

"First place: Alberto Grestini...No fucking way! Come on, it is not possible...That bastard has screwed me over again, I deeply hate him!"

I was happy with the result obtained, and at the same time I was sick to death that Alberto himself had beaten me, but, after all, it would be a pleasure to go together. Elisa hugged me tightly, congratulating me, with a veiled sadness on her face.

"It's incredible to think that many people had been preparing for months and you, finding out about it the day before, you came second... You really piss me off, I want to slap you! I don't know how you get away with it every time, but you're phenomenal, I must admit it; you amaze me more and more every day! Congratulations Oliver..."

She hadn't even made it to the top twenty and for one of the few times, I had felt sincere sorrow for someone else. I knew how much she cared, and I wish she had won too.

"Tell you what, you keep studying and working hard and I will hire you one day at my newspaper. After all, if it wasn't for you, I would have never even entered this contest. And I never forget the people who help me. Deal?!"

"Deal!"

Her face finally became more relaxed. A few moments later my phone rang:

"Hello?"

"OLIVEEEEEEEERR!!!!!" Alberto's big voice echoed in my eardrum, making me jump.

"So, what do you say?! Take it home!!!"

"You are a cuckold! I don't know who you paid to get ahead of me, but it is a good contact to have! However, I am happy to be able to continue together. Like the old days!"

"Haha! You're the usual idiot!! See you in London, my friend! See you soon!"

6.

I had not yet realised what had happened. I went home and told my father the news, who was proudly surprised but also worried:

"Good boy, you really impressed me this time. But tell me, how are you going to support yourself for a month in London? Unfortunately, I have no money to give you".

"I have some savings to spare", I answered.

"Bravo, go and waste them all in an unpaid internship, to learn how to do a job that doesn't even pay rent, if not to just a handful of people with connections, without so much as a hint of a degree in your hand? Oliver, I would love for you to go if things were different, but there comes a time in life when you have to face reality. A position at the cookie factory is about to open up, old Elmo is about to retire. With a little push, maybe I can get you in..."

“I hate those fucking cookies!”

"It may not be the most rewarding job in the world, but it guarantees you a salary with which to build a decent life. And then it's a permanent contract. Time is running out and it's a great opportunity!”

"How beautiful! Forty years in the factory making cookies! With excellent career possibilities in case somebody dies or retires! That's exactly what I always dreamed of as a child!"

"You don't want to understand. This is real life! It's made of sweat, fatigue and dirty hands, whether you like it or not, you have to get over it!"

I remained silent for a few seconds.

"Dad...Are you happy?"

"Well...." he hesitated, "In the end we are not so badly-off. Happiness is a relative concept."

"I am sorry that you think so, and I can understand why, nor do I judge you for it, because you have all the reasons in the world. But for me it is not yet time to give up. I cannot think that life is reduced only to work, to making someone else rich off my back, working twelve hours a day to pay my bills and sleep. Not like that, without even trying. If I fail, I promise you that I will make my peace and I will come and knead cookies with you, but not now. I still believe in it and I want to go through with it".

My father lowered his eyes in a disconsolate manner. I was sure he could understand me, but he probably wanted to test the extent to which I was really determined to push myself.

The summer months leading up to my move went by quickly, between occasional chores, a few friends and many beers, with only one thought in my head.

Then, on the twenty-fifth of October, the day had finally arrived. I had never been out of Italy before and the idea excited me. My father walked me to the airport to the check-in desk. He would never admit it, but there was sadness in his eyes. I was sorry to leave him alone, but a life in the cookie factory just wasn't for me.

Before saying goodbye, he put his hand in his pocket and pulled out a bunch of bills:

"This is all I have saved in the last six months, it's not much, but at least you wouldn't be on the street. And take these cookies too, in case you get hungry."

It was his way of telling me that he loved me and maybe, after all, a part of him hoped that I would make it, to redeem his life as well. He didn't want to say it out loud, because you know, even dreaming has a price and he didn't want any more disappointments in his life. We said goodbye with a firm but heartfelt embrace.

"... Please be careful..." was all he was able to say with his slightly teary eyes. I had them too, but we were both too "manly" to admit it to one another. We both knew that, although the internship was only for a month, I was going there to stay and there was a good chance that we would not see each other for a long time. As I was about to pass security, I heard his voice in the distance:

"Good luck son!! Show them what you're worth!"

A slight smile spread across his face, mixed with a spark of hope in his watery eyes. I waved at him, turned around and wiped my eyes then headed for the gate. I had never been on a plane before. I sat by the window, I watched the city shrinking in size, fascinated, until I arrived suspended a few meters above an immense white expanse of clouds. I could see the blue-greyness of the sky at the end of the day, mixed with the colours of a pale sunset, surrounded only by irregular shaped clouds, barely glimpsing the artificial glow of the city below.

"We are now landing at London Stansted."

The captain's hoarse voice echoed through the speakers. Suddenly, I felt the plane descending sharply, seeing the surrounding whiteness that had enveloped me so far had faded away. The shapes, those dark and magical colours of eight o'clock in the evening and the set of lights gradually became clearer and more distinct. The side flaps opened and shortly after a small thud, we had landed.

“Finally, we are here,” I thought to myself.

My dream started from there. I found myself at Stansted airport, pierced by an icy wind that went straight through me and a thin drizzle that slowly drenched me without me even really noticing.

I took my luggage and jumped on the first available bus. It was already eleven o'clock in the evening when I arrived in Hammersmith. I was fascinated by the very different environment, by the smells of the take-aways, by the riverside and by the lights of the bridge, which created a magical and melancholic atmosphere, a reality that I had never tasted before. I stopped by the river to smoke a cigarette, sitting on the wall. I was happy and open to the new world of which I was about to become a part of. And just like in Rome, a guy came to bum a cigarette off me.

His name was Lukasz, or something similar, and he was Polish. I found out that he also had a room in my new home nearby. He was a bricklayer and had been living there for a year, also trying his luck. Our house had five bedrooms and only one bathroom; it was the classic Victorian house, spanning three floors. I could smell the typical scent of old and musty places. It was completely covered with a brown carpet, at least ten years old, which had probably seen a lot of people coming and going.

My room was a third of an attic, a small hole with just

enough place for a coffee table and a single bed, squashed in the corner. I paid around five hundred pounds a month, about the cost of a studio apartment on the outskirts of Rome. I hit my head on the ceiling a couple of times and some debris came down, but I tried not to worry about it. I put my bags down and decided to go for a ride downtown.

Life in London was much faster than in Italy. They all ran, even on the escalators of the subway, where, among other things, the seats were also covered with carpet and which was of an efficiency never known before: there were thirteen lines that connected the city and trains that passed every two minutes. Rome's public transport seemed light years away.

As soon as I got out of the underground, I found myself observing the spectacle that is the River Thames, illuminated by the Ferris wheel of the London Eye and framed by Big Ben. The whole thing had something magical and mysterious to offer. I opened a beer and sat down to enjoy the show. Even if I didn't know it yet, it would always remain a place to call home.

7.

The next morning, I woke up early and set off for my first day at the Times.

The office was located within the London Bridge district, near the bridge of the same name. I arrived well in advance and decided to go for breakfast. I went into a cafe that also served English breakfast. I met Alberto, who was already getting high. On his plate were two eggs, three strips of smoked bacon and four sausages, with a side dish of baked beans and chips.

"Hey Oliver! You're here too?! I don't know about you, but I already love this country!", he exclaimed smugly. I got a toastie and an espresso, probably the worst I had ever drank, and sat down next to him. Once he had stuffed everything but the plates in his face, we finally made our way to the offices of the Times. As soon as we entered the building, the girl at the reception desk, who was wearing a miniskirt so short and tight that it left very little room for imagination, accompanied us to our meeting room. There were about ten of us, the ones from the contest plus the other six who were awarded with the same opportunity and two queue jumpers, just there due to their connections. We also met Eleonora, the third runner-up, who had already been there for half an hour. Alberto and I introduced ourselves, but she was so sour that she barely looked at us.

“Please, show some respect, we even ranked higher than you!" I whispered jokingly to Alberto, who broke out in a thunderous laugh that made her even more upset.

Shortly after a series of interesting characters entered, very well-dressed but with bright ties and socks that were a sartorial slap in the face. They gave us a brief introduction on the details of the internship and ended with great news:

"As you know, our newspaper cooperates with our Italian partner and the purpose of this experience is to train you, and then hire one of you as a foreign correspondent, collaborating directly with Mr Mutti, here beside me. So, work hard and may the best person win!".

Wow, I had no idea. It was a fantastic opportunity, and, without a doubt, an internal war would ensue to get the job.

The following days were very hard at work and everything required twice as much mental effort. I was trying hard anyway, even if the forced cohabitation with strangers did not help me and the conditions were certainly not the best. In my room, when it rained heavily (which in London was not a rare occurrence), water dripped from the ceiling.

The Poles smoked continuously, making the air stale. One afternoon we had finished sooner than usual, thus I came home early to find one of them shagging some random girl on the kitchen table, as his friend in the room was busy with another one. Absolutely extraordinary.

Also, my savings were starting to run out. At lunch I had a chocolate bar and for dinner, whatever I could find. I often went to Alberto's house, where I could always get a plate of pasta somehow. For the first time, I really understood what my father meant; it was a real struggle for survival, further amplified by the fact that I had no family to rely on, except those few friends who, thank God, were never lacking.

The next morning, after an intense three-hour session on the careful hunt for credible news sources to write about, I began to explore the newspaper's archives. A photo from a few years earlier caught my attention. It was an article about a case of corruption and money laundering, perpetrated by a certain Adrian Floberti, back then, the director of Solus Era, an innovative software company based in Turin at the time.

I learned about that company, discovering that it was taken over by a British multinational and later sold to a Korean investment group, a company called Kaiwon. I read that, despite the obvious guilt, Floberti was acquitted for lack of evidence.

The thing that struck me the most about that article, however, was the photo, in particular the woman who appeared in the background. I could not say exactly, and it was also a bit blurry but...it looked a lot like the memory I had of my mother. I tried to do some more research about it, but could not find out anything concrete.

"Oliver I'm starving, are you coming?"

Without giving it too much thought, I went with Alberto to lunch.

The month of internship passed quickly, and it was time for the final test. It was a cold day and London was all decorated with many lights and colours. Alberto and I hugged each other quickly for support as we entered the offices of the Times.

"Good luck, man. You know, it's between you and me. Whoever wins, pulls the other one up!"

"Are you afraid of losing? You must be, because this time I won't let you have it!!

He laughed and took his place.

They brought us the instructions for the article that we were to write and, shortly afterwards, we began. This time I was nervous, the stakes were high, and I couldn't concentrate.

"Excuse me sir...!", exclaimed the person in charge with a stern tone, which was addressed to Alberto.

He was munching a salami sandwich while scribbling on some paper.

"I don't work well on an empty stomach!"

Everyone burst out laughing and the atmosphere became more relaxed. Finally, my pen began to flow.

I came home exhausted and hungry. I saw a mouse coming out from under the stove and then crawling under the door. I had lost the desire to cook, so I walked down to a nearby pub.

To hell with it, whichever way it was going to go, that night I had to celebrate. After the third pint of IPA, I went out to smoke a cigarette. I met Charlotte, an English girl who worked at an employment agency and she gave me the numbers of a couple of contacts.

We were both pretty drunk and, after a short casual conversation, we ended up doing it in the pub bathroom. When it was over, she pulled up her pants and left smiling, without even saying goodbye.

It's really true that everything goes faster in London.

8.

The next day, I immediately set out to look for a job. The results of the test at the Times would not arrive until after Christmas and I didn't have much hope anyway. In addition, I was almost broke.

London is one of the most expensive cities in the world and you end up spending money even if you stand still; I could have asked my father for some money, but I knew he didn't even have enough for himself and I didn't want to make things difficult for him. It was my choice and I had to make it on my own.

I handed out two hundred CVs in five days, walking through the city.

After a week, I received a call from the world's most famous fast-food chain for an interview in Notting Hill. It went well and I started the first day of training. My supervisor was an Indian guy, a bit smug and disinterested. He showed me the hot plate where I had to cook the frozen hamburgers, the basket where I had to prepare the fries and the various compartments containing the condiments. It was as hot as hell in that kitchen and every time I put something in to fry, hot oil splashed all over me. The only protection we had was a disposable plastic glove, which would sometimes melt, leaving bits on the burger or the grill, but he didn't seem to care. I noticed that he had numerous burns on his arms and asked him what had happened.

"It's nothing, I've been here for a year, you'll get used to it too," he said without giving it much importance.

The first impression was certainly not the best. After not even an hour, he asked me to change the oil in the fryer. As I was walking with the container in my hand, hot oil splashed on my arm and slipped, pouring it onto the grill, culminating in a small fire. The alarm went off and we were forced to evacuate the building. Everyone was looking at me angrily. When everything was resolved, after the fire brigade intervened, the boss wanted to see me in his office.

"Not bad for the first day, no one had ever managed to burn down the store before!"

"I'm sorry, I didn't do it on purpose."

"I am sure; however, I do not think it is wise for both of us to continue. You will be paid for the day, but I'm afraid I can't continue letting you work here".

"I understand. Thank you and goodbye."

I wasn't particularly sorry to have lost that job, even though my economic problems were still there and I had to find a solution as soon as possible.

I was on my way home, when I suddenly received a call from an Italian pizzeria, also located in Notting Hill. The manager's name was Daniel, a guy from South Italy, in his mid-thirties. He asked me if I was available for a trial run that evening and I happily accepted. Fortunately, I had a spare black shirt with me, so I immediately took the bus in the opposite direction and reached the pizzeria.

I still smelled like fried food and wasn't very presentable, but I seemed to make a good impression, especially with my level of English. I had never worked in a restaurant before and I was really unsure what to do, but I put a lot of effort into learning fast.

It was seven o'clock in the evening and I hadn't eaten since the day before; I was starting to feel dizzy. So, even though I was a little ashamed of it, while I was throwing away the leftovers from the dishes I was clearing, I ate what seemed the most edible. A table had left half a fried chicken cutlet, a piece of buffalo mozzarella and a slice of margherita pizza, which I devoured in less than a minute. Then I went to get the tiramisu glasses from the refrigerator downstairs and I took a couple. It had been a long time since I had eaten so well!

Having said that, working in that place became quite hellish. Daniel was hooked on coke and spent his evenings yelling at everyone, often smashing dishes on the floor, pushing us to the brink.

I had only been there for three weeks, but it felt like a lifetime. Fortunately, the pay was weekly, which gave me a breather and allowed me to pay another month's rent.

I finally had a day off, which I spent drinking, shopping, doing the washing and cleaning the house. Then in the evening, around midnight, I received an unexpected call from my colleague Laura, who was sobbing:

"Oliver...That bastard laid us off...you, me and Andrew. To hire his friends. He told me to let you know."

I was speechless. I was certainly not one of the best waiters around, but I was doing my part. It was quite unfair. I called the restaurant immediately. The asshole was still inside, probably snorting a few ounces in his office, and answered with his usual, false, slimy tone:

"Hello Hello Metro Pizza!"

"You don't even have the balls to say it to my face?"

"...I didn't have your number...", he only managed to stutter.

“What a great manager you are! You don’t even have the number of your employees!"

He hung up. And I was unemployed again.

Before I was laid off, I had managed to get four days off,

so I decided, with the little money I had earned, to go home and spend Christmas with my father. I had booked exactly four days, thinking I would then have to go back to work.

It was December twenty-fourth. I arrived at Rome Ciampino airport around six in the evening, my father was supposed to pick me up at that time. But when I left the terminal, no one was there. After half an hour I tried to call him, but his cell phone had been disconnected. I lit a cigarette and sat down to wait. After an hour and a half, my phone rang.

"Good evening, are you the son of Ettore Milani?"

"I am…"

"...I'm sorry boy...Unfortunately yours is the only number we could find, I'm sorry you have to find out this way. Your father was in a serious car accident and passed away a few hours ago".

Those words stuck my chest like a blade. I couldn't even cry.

I sat down for another two hours; I couldn't understand it. I was pale in the face and freezing cold, but I couldn't feel it. A distinguished gentleman, who had just accompanied his son, saw me and took me for coffee. His name was Oreste. After telling him everything, he had the good heart to accompany me to the hospital and wait with me so I could do all the paperwork.

"Come to dinner at my house tonight, it is not nice to be alone on Christmas Eve".

"I don't want to be a bother"

"No bother, I'm on my own and your company can only please me."

"Why are you doing all this for me? You don't even know me"

"Because I have a son your age and I would like to think that, if he ever found himself in your situation, even in such a world of intolerant bastards which we are living in, there would be at least one who would do the right thing."

Oreste prepared a hearty dinner, but I couldn't eat much for obvious reasons. It seemed so surreal that it had happened to me. I wasn't able to feel anything. And I was also starting to feel guilty about it. I was not prepared to deal with the pain so suddenly and it was as if a self-defence mechanism had been triggered, putting a lock on my feelings and emotions.

I stayed at Oreste's, in his son's room, but I didn't sleep a wink all night.

On Christmas day, he gave me a ride to my father's house. As soon as I passed the threshold, I breathed in his smell and saw his things scattered around. I felt a strong pain in the pit of my stomach, and I went to the bathroom to vomit.

I began to be bombarded with calls and messages from people I hadn't seen or heard from in years, who were sending me their condolences, but I didn't want to hear from anyone and I turned off my phone. I sat there in my own world, staring into the void. So, I went to get a case of beer and a case of whiskey from my father's pantry and started drinking, one after the other, all the bottles that were there, until I collapsed exhausted on the couch.

A figure made its way through the semi-darkness, which

seemed familiar to me. My father appeared and smiled at me.

"What the fuck are you smiling at, is this the way to leave, just like that, without saying goodbye? Are you leaving me here alone?"

"There is a reason for everything. Be strong. Don't worry about me, I'm fine here. Let go of the guilt. It's nobody's fault, it was supposed to go like this."

"What do I do now, Dad? I feel lost...", I sobbed with a little voice.

"You already know what you must do. Go and finish what you have started..."

"I have no more money, no job and soon I won't even have a house to go back to, neither here nor there. I'm trying hard, but it's a constant struggle out there, I don't know if I can do it..."

"Oliver...I never doubted that you could do it. You're almost there. Keep on following the path you feel inside".

"You are the one who offered me a job at the cookie

factory!"

"If you've reconsidered, a place has just opened up!" he laughed.

His image became blurrier.

"Wait, I still have things to ask you, are you leaving me here like this?!", I shouted at him with a lost look.

"Forgive me if I have always been so distant, but know that I love you very much. Since you left, there hasn't been a day that I haven't thought about you or bragged about you to my colleagues. There is something that'll help, in the third drawer in the kitchen, which I did not have time to give you. I am very proud of you son. Always with your head held high, you'll make it. I have to go now. Keep your strength up, I am close to you, always! Merry Christmas Oliver."

Smiling, he left.

9.

Still a little foggy, I opened my eyes and found myself in the hospital sitting on the bed and intubated. Had it been a dream, a figment of my imagination, like Dumbledore for Harry Potter? That conversation seemed so vivid though.

"He is awake!" shouted the nurse. The doctor entered the room and approached me with a stern look.

"Boy, how much have you had to drink? You went into an alcohol-induced coma! What were you thinking? I don't know by what miracle you're here to tell the tale! If that gentleman had not brought you here in time, you would have been dead".

I turned around. There was Oreste at the door.

"...But how...?"

"I was on the couch watching television, watching one of

those Christmas *variety* shows that makes you cry more than laugh. While I was wondering if you were all right, a box of chocolate cookies fell on my head from the cupboard, and I took it as a sign."

I looked above with a smile.

"I am not superstitious, but I decided to get in the car, given the already difficult situation. In fact, after knocking five times, the neighbour, who had an extra set of keys, came out and we found you lying on the couch".

"...I thank you. From the bottom of my heart. I saw my father...", I said, still a little confused.

"Eh, I believe it, you were more dead than alive! In any case, I hope he told you what he had to say to you," he replied, accentuating a smile.

"Now get some rest, if it suits you, you'll be back in shape by New Year's Eve!", he joked.

"Thanks again for everything. Merry Christmas, Oreste."

I stayed there another night and was discharged the next

day. Still a little bit upside down, I headed home. I was still not well, in every aspect, but I couldn't even afford to stay still. While I was trying to think what to do, I remembered that conversation with my father. Maybe I had imagined it all and it was just what I wanted to hear. Yet I remembered everything perfectly. With low expectations, I went into the kitchen and opened the third drawer. There was an envelope with five hundred euros inside and a note: 'A little help for a great goal. Continue to pursue your dream. Merry Christmas, your proud dad.'

I finally burst into a deep and liberating cry, after which, exhausted, I fell asleep.

It took me a couple of weeks to organise everything that had resulted from my father's passing. The landlord told me that the rent for that month had not been paid, but given the situation, he did not insist. My father had left me the money for his rent. I gave him back the keys to the apartment and took the bus to the airport, heading to London.

My single room and the Polish bricklayers were in the same

state of decay as I had left them. One of them greeted me with a loud "WELCOME BACK"!! burping while drinking yet another beer.

I had five hundred euros in my pocket, twenty days' rent paid and felt hopeless.

I put down my suitcase and walked to the nearest bureau de change. The best one I knew was located in Queensway, an Arab neighbourhood near Paddington and Hyde Park. After exchanging the money, I decided to go for a walk to clear my head. I saw three hooded guys following me. I tried to change my route, but they caught up and surrounded me.

"Wallet and cell phone, pull out everything, you piece of shit".

"I'd rather get killed, now get the fuck out of here."

It wasn't about the money. That was the last gift from my father, I would not have given it to him for anything in the world.

"Oh, what a brave little boy!" The taller one approached me and headbutted me so hard that he split my left eyebrow open. The guy next to me, kicked me in the stomach, which made me bend over. Once on the ground, all three of them started kicking and punching me, until two of them were able to immobilise me and open my jacket to take out my wallet. Not happy, the bastard pulled out a switchblade and put it to my throat, mimicking with his thumb that he was going to slit my throat.

'So that's how it ends', I thought a little disappointed.

Suddenly, two hands grabbed him by the throat from behind. I couldn't really see very well what was going on, all I saw was some six and a half feet guy being tossed against a wall with his arm bent in half, screaming and writhing in pain. I managed to focus: Alberto!

The other two left me to go over him. He was in a fury. He slapped the first one who fell to the ground and punched the other one right in his mouth, who then tried to fight back, making Alberto even angrier and in his rage, he threw his opponent in a dumpster. "And be thankful that I didn't find a manhole, because idiots like you belong in the sewer!"

He picked up my wallet and helped me up. My eyebrow

was bleeding and I was a little bruised, but compared to those three I was fine. I had never seen Alberto so enraged. Luckily for me, he arrived at the right time.

"Thanks Alby, it's good to see you again".

"Shitty people. Let's leave before I kill them all, I'll get you something to eat."

The next day, still sore, I was awakened by the vibration of my cell phone. It was an email from the Times. I opened it and started to scroll quickly.

'Dear Mr. Milani, we thank you for your participation and your hard work.

Despite your brilliance, professionalism and undisputed skills, we are sorry to inform you that you do not meet the necessary requirements to continue with us. We wish you the best of luck in your journalistic career.

Best regards.'

'Perfect, it gets better and better', I thought. I kept staring at the phone sleepily. I had believed it, for a while. A few minutes later, I received a message from Alberto:

"Hey Oliver, what's up?"

"It went wrong. I suppose it's the same for you..."

"...Yes...", he replied, disheartened.

"Beer in Soho?"

"Beer it is. See you at four o'clock in the usual place."

Soho was perhaps the most central neighbourhood in London, near Piccadilly Circus. It was very much frequented by the gay community and had some very picturesque places. I arrived on time and saw Alberto a few meters away, waiting for me at the entrance of the pub; just in time to enjoy the scene:

"What a cuddly teddy bear!", exclaimed an extremely effeminate bald individual with a Village People moustache, giving Alberto a pat on the ass. He, surprised and terrified, snapped back, ending up bumping into a girl with a tray full of pints of beer, which shattered into a thousand pieces.

I couldn't stop laughing and he turned purple in the face with shame, so we decided to move to another place a little quieter.

We walked to "*Shakespeare's Head*", a typical English pub with wooden tables and a filthy carpet at least thirty years old. We ordered two beers and sat down. Alberto looked sombre.

"I didn't expect to win when I came here, but it's always bad when you wake up from a good dream."

"I know. What will you do now?"

"...Oliver...Let's look at the reality. It's good to dream and it was right to try. But it's time to go home. I don't have a job and I'm almost out of money myself. I'm tired of eating shit, sharing a house with godless lunatics and going out every day with an umbrella. I'm going back to Italy the day after tomorrow and I'm going to help my father. I am lucky enough to have at least one guaranteed job. What is your plan?"

"I don't know. I don't have anything anymore. But somehow, I will manage. I don't know why, but I feel that I have to stay here".

"Good luck then... If you need anything, you know you only have to ask..."

"You've already done so much, including all the dinners you shared with me when I had an empty fridge and wallet. I don't know what I would have done without you here. I will always remember that."

After my words, I noticed a hint of emotion in his gaze, which he immediately averted.

"It was a pleasure to be in your company. I'll send you some wild boar salami when I get back".

I laughed.

"Do not beat yourself up, Alby. One day I will have my newspaper and hire you to work with me. You will always remain my worthy rival!" I joked.

We finished the last sip and hugged each other. In fact, he squeezed me almost to the point where my lungs were in my throat.

"Bye, cuddly teddy bear!"

He gave me a melancholy smile and left.

10.

The next morning, I went to a private employment agency, located in the then infamous Seven Sisters neighbourhood.

It was run by Italians and had a joining fee of fifty pounds. I saw a little group of people waiting for a call. Most of the jobs they were offering were in the restaurant business, which to me was shit, as well as myself being incapable and inexperienced in that field. I only had on my side, compared to most of the others, a decent level of English.

After a couple of hours spent sitting and waiting, the owner, a Sicilian woman named Anna in her fifties, called me for an interview. I was honest and revealed to her that I did not have much experience, but I emphasised that I had lots of goodwill. She sent me to a very futuristic restaurant near Waterloo, just a stone's throw from the Thames, for a trial run as an assistant barman.

It was a total disaster. I also studied all the cocktails and the wine list before going there, but my supervisor, also Italian, did everything to get me into trouble, to test how I would react. Maybe because he was also a bit of an asshole.

I polished at least five hundred glasses during that test, I broke two and prepared a Bellini with tomato juice and a Bloody Mary with Prosecco. The highlight of the evening was when he asked me to open a bottle of sparkling wine without making any noise. My hands were wet and I had lost some of my sensitivity after having washed so many glasses, so, in addition to making noise, the cork flung off, which ended up hitting the floppy breast of a heavily overweight old woman, who began to yell at me, enraged. After witnessing the whole thing, the manager walked me to the door.

I went back to the agency the next day. Anna sent me to another Italian restaurant in Angel, with a ridiculous name. It was called “La Pancetta”. I was already imagining the prestige I would have got from the remote possibility of being hired. "Where do you work?" "At La Pancetta!"

I accepted anyway. I was in no condition to refuse anything.

I lasted a week there, but also met some interesting guys. I was the youngest of the group and, let’s say that, while in my previous experience I was almost invisible, at least here they were greeting me and shared few words. All the waiters were Italians, however, none of them, normally, used to really do that job. The crisis in Italy was spreading and many had decided to seek their fortune in London.

I met Enrico, a former Italian actor and Bossa Nova singer, also from Turin, who was quite cynical and critical of everyone and of life in general. Then there was a woman in her forties, Elsa. Nice and haughty at the same time, who had been designing jewellery in Genoa and couldn't admit she didn't make it. There was Alfredo, a Neapolitan guy who dealt coke and had fun breaking the mirrors off parked cars. And then there was me, looking for an unexpected stability. It was the perfect picture of the new emigrants of our century, who, for some reason still unclear, life had brought them there.

Although the work did not excite me, it was pleasant to have someone "familiar" to talk to and this was my daily motivation.

Then one day an Arab tourist came to eat with us, asking me for advice on which appetiser to order, in an incomprehensible English, telling me that he wanted to make a good impression on his girlfriend, a girl wearing a burka who must have been half his age. I brought them a plate of mixed cold cuts. While she was insatiably swallowing two slices of raw meat, he suspected it was pork and I suspected I was fired. We were both right.

I went back to the agency again and this time I was sent to an office cleaning company.

I felt I had really hit rock bottom. Not that there was anything wrong with that job, but it was definitely different from my initial expectations. Eight hours dusting furniture, desks, floors. And the toilets. One night we were cleaning Ealing's city council building and there was putrid water coming out of the men's room. Obviously, they sent me, the rookie. I went into that toilet overflowing with shit. I had to stick my hand down the bottom of the toilet to pull out a six-inch soft turd which had clogged everything, but during the operation my latex glove had come off and I found myself with the aforementioned turd in my bare hands, holding back the vomit.

All this for five pounds an hour. I lasted three weeks in that cleaning company, after which they told me that they were out of work, and I was almost relieved. I'd raised enough money for another month's rent and a few packs of sausages from Tesco, the most popular supermarket chain. Six sausages for fifty pence, with as much as forty percent meat, dripping in an unknown orange colour liquid, banned from the market nowadays.

I missed the dinners at Alberto's and my friends in general, I felt incredibly lonely and had a great desire to blow everything up and run away.

11.

At the agency I met Pier, a guy who had, like me, escaped from everyday life in the suburbs of Rome, in search of a more fulfilling one.

He was an interesting guy, maybe a little crazy, and we had many things in common: we were both ambitious, penniless and we liked women a lot. But compared to me, Pier was phenomenal: he changed jobs every month, but it was his choice. He was a very smart and positive person and he always managed to get in his employer's good books.

We started going out often and we created a good friendship, based on mutual respect. Despite our financial constraints, it was always a great night out: we used to buy ourselves a couple of cans of nine percent beer at the "off licence", a sort of mini-market present in every district of

London, and then tried to pick up girls in the most degraded free clubs.

Once he was so drunk that he started dancing with a Slovakian woman in her sixties and, lost in the moment, he took her to the bathroom. I saw him come out shortly afterwards with a serious look, asking me to go out for a smoke. I followed him.

"...Well...?"

"Oh Oliver...We were about to finish up, then I pulled down her panties...I saw a forest of silvery pubic hair, and I couldn't make it!"

"HAHA! WHAT AN ASSHOLE!"

Another time it was even worse for him. He had managed to pick up a girl who looked like a supermodel, or at least, she looked like one after four beers. She was Brazilian and was twenty-two years old; angelic face, very busty and charming, but there was something about her that didn't convince me.

"Oliver, tonight I fell in love!"

"She is absolutely beautiful...But isn't that a bit strange?"

"What is?"

"That someone like that would leave with one of us?"

"But what are you saying? I already told her that I’m out of money. She only wanted someone to accompany her home. And then, come on! I'm a good-looking guy, she's going to want some quality after who knows how many dried-up dicks she's used to!"

I saw him getting on the night bus with her. I didn't hear from him for a week, until he asked me out again, telling me that he needed to talk to me. We met near Big Ben, opened a can of beer and sat on the wall, smoking. He was a little bit bummed out.

"What happened?"

"Do you remember the girl from the other night?"

"Of course I do. How did it go?"

"...We went to her house and she offered me some more drinks. After a couple of drinks, she took me into the bedroom, and she bent over..."

"...Wow... She certainly isn't someone who would make you beg for it!"

"Eh...so basically...we started having sex, then after a few minutes I realised something was different... Frozen in place, I shout at her, "BUT ARE YOU A MAN!?"

She stops, and with a deep and low voice, she says to me “AND WHAT WERE YOU EXPECTING??”. I didn't know what to do, and I tried to run away from her, but she...or rather, he, had locked the door, holding the keys hostage in the bedside table".

I was trying to show understanding, struggling to hold myself back. I almost had tears in my eyes from laughter, but I tried to keep quiet, holding my breath for a few seconds.

"I tried to grab the keys, but the asshole was so strong, he threw me on the bed and started whipping me in the face with his dick, shouting “DO YOU LIKE IT?!” And saying that I was his bitch," he continued, more and more upset; "I was really afraid of getting fucked!"

At that point I couldn't hold back any longer and I burst out laughing, hunched over, just imagining the scene and he started laughing too, even though I could still see the terror in his eyes.

"I managed to break the lock by kicking it and I ran away, while the guy was holding me from behind and clutching me with his size 13 feet around my thighs. When I got home, I washed my penis with bleach and spent a week walking around the bars, telling strangers how traumatised I was. What a bad experience!"

"HAHAHA!! I AM DYING!!!"

"You laugh, asshole, it'll happen to you too, sooner or later! You never know who you're going to end up with!"

Yes, the beauty (or, in some cases, the ugliness) of London was also this, you never know where it will take you, or with whom, especially at night.

12.

My registration period with the agency had expired and I would have had to pay another fifty pounds, which I did not have.

I sat in a cafe and had a coffee. The girl who served it to me had an impatient face and barely spoke to me, not even a hello.

I've never put up with that kind of attitude, in fact, I get annoyed a lot. You can have all the best reasons, but it costs nothing to be nice, or at least polite. By now, I was surprised when I noticed a minimum of humanity around people, I was even almost moved when someone stopped in front of the crosswalk to let me cross the street. Who knows why; it takes much more effort to be rude for no reason, and you live badly.

Anyway, I noticed that they were looking for a bartender and I kindly asked her who I could leave my resume with. Luckily for me (or at least, in that circumstance), she was the manager of the store. She gave me a quick interview and I was hired on trial basis, starting the following week.

In the meantime, my home contract had expired and I had to move out, which was fortunate. I got a room in Dollis Hill, a not-so-recommendable neighbourhood in zone three in northwest London, in a house with fifteen other people.

To tell the truth, it looked more like a hostel than a house, populated by Italians and Brazilians. After some time, we became like a big family; it was also nice to come back in the evening and have a chat with friends.

The cafeteria where I started working opened at six and was located forty minutes by bus from my new home, which meant I had to get up at four in the morning.

Every morning, at that bus stop, it was always just me and a Romanian guy talking on the phone all the time; who knows who the fuck he was talking to at that time. It was February and there was always a goddamn icy wind, so after a week, I had a fever.

However, I didn't miss a single day. I really wanted to keep that job. It was not the best life had to offer, but I preferred making coffee to cleaning dishes and glasses and the atmosphere of the place was not bad, except when the manager was on duty with me.

Her name was Lydia, she was pretty, but for some reason she was always pissed off at the world.

Although I got bronchitis and could barely stand up, I was always there and did my best. The trial month passed quickly and Lydia called me into her office.

"Dear Oliver...you are an acceptable bartender, but I have to finish your probationary period here."

"And why is that?"

"You don't smile enough when you serve customers, service is important in this company."

I thought she was joking, but come to think of it, she never joked. Fired because I wasn't smiling enough. And by her of all people! I didn't want to believe it. I looked at the ceiling for a moment, wondering what I was doing wrong and why I couldn't get it right. I took my things and walked out of the store, swearing while blowing a sarcastic kiss goodbye in response to her with thirty-two teeth smile.

I came home disconsolate, telling my roommates, who were also in disbelief, what had happened.

I was miserably penniless again, but I didn't lose heart.

A few days later, I got a call from an Italian ice cream shop in Portobello, a picturesque neighbourhood in the centre of Notting Hill, right next to the famous library from the Julia Roberts and Hugh Grant movie. That area was somehow lucky for me, I was already on the third job I could get around here.

Compared to all the others I had done, it was a piece of cake: I sold about ten ice creams a day, I ate as many as I wanted and, the rest of the time, I spent on the computer minding my own business. After all, there were not many people eager for an ice cream in London in March.

I finally managed to find some economic stability; I could not consider myself fulfilled, but I had a moment of breathing space.

I stayed and "worked" there for six months, until the time came for the famous Jamaican carnival in August. It was an annual event of three days, with a strong turnout of people of Caribbean and African-American origin, who were wasting themselves with beer, weed, acid and jerk chicken, smashing everything they found.

For this reason, practically all the stores on Portobello were closed during that event. All except ours, since the owner had the brilliant idea to leave it open to compensate for the lack of turnover in recent months.

That Sunday I saw hell on earth. It was a never-ending march of these drunken, half naked, folkloristic beasts who made their way through the crowd, advancing like animals in heat between the parade floats, pumping deafening and unlistenable music.

Around three o'clock in the afternoon, there were already more drunk and stoned than sober, with imaginable results: people pissing and vomiting everywhere, streets clogged, people collapsed on the corners sleeping in their vomit. And of course, they stormed the store. They went in and emptied the cash register, smashed a window, shat on the stairs and two of them began fucking on the ice cream machine, leaving the used condom on the mint chocolate chip gelato reserve as a souvenir. I called the police, but they arrived after six hours, when everything was already destroyed.

"Oh wow, looks like they had a good time here. There's not much we can do at the moment," said one of them, without showing any particular interest;

"Do me a favour, kid, it's been a bad day...Could you make me a cup of coffee?

I would have thrown the coffee in his face, but I indulged him.

That was my last day of work in that ice-cream parlour, which closed its doors for good; the damage was considerable and the owner, who had rented the place, decided he didn't want to invest another penny in it.

At least I had set something aside in those six months and I could live quietly for some time, while I was looking for another job.

I had lost my job again, but I didn't care all that much. It had been almost a year since I had arrived in London and it seemed like a lifetime ago. It had been a hard, intense year, always on the edge, and I had also lost my father. However, I was making it; slowly my new life began to take shape.

I had no idea where this tangled road was leading me, but, in the meantime, I was moving on; it was certainly less monotonous than my Italian daily life.

Besides, I had rediscovered a little bit of humanity in people even in the face of a cynical society rampant with indifference. I had never been in a situation like this before, nor have I ever been particularly religious, but I learned that when you give everything, a hand, from somewhere, always comes to you, even when all seems lost.

13.

I was very tired emotionally and I decided I needed a change of scenery for a while. I would have liked to see Alberto and Elisa again, but I was not yet ready to return to Rome; the memory of the last time was still vivid in my mind and I needed some space.

I opted for Japan. The Far East had always fascinated me and seemed like the perfect place to relax, away from the frenzy of London.

Back home, I started looking for offers and booked a flight for the next day. I packed my suitcase and set the alarm for four hours later.

I don't know how long I had slept that night, probably around twenty minutes. My head was crowded with thoughts. Anyway, I took a quick shower to wake up, put on my pants and headed towards Heathrow airport.

My final destination was Osaka, with a stopover in Rome for a couple of hours, where I managed to enjoy a decent espresso after a long time. I was so happy that I had three coffees within those two hours.

The plane was full of Japanese, there were only three Italians, probably due to the fact that many preferred to go to Tokyo. As chance would have it, I sat right next to one of them. His name was Gianmarco and he was going to an international congress of lawyers. Apparently, he was a big shot in the business, but he was also a rather weary person and I was dying to sleep. While he was telling me about his dazzling career and the thousands of business trips that had allowed him to travel the world, I collapsed on the seat and woke up only to the thud of the wheels landing on the runway.

No one spoke English at all, but they had a kindness I had never known before. I showed the piece of paper with the reservation of my hotel and was accompanied by an airport employee to the train platform.

I had managed to figure out which stop I had to change at, but not which train to take to get to my destination. I asked a girl for help, who, seeing the train leaving, told the controller to wait for me until I got on. I waved to her from the window trying to thank her, while she was accompanying me with her eyes, showing off a big smile.

When I arrived at my destination, there was an immense expanse of buildings, signs and a thousand streets full of colours that intertwined with each other. I didn't have a smartphone at the time, nor Google Maps, so I didn't know where to start. I asked for help outside a supermarket and an old man came to my rescue. After reading the name of the hotel, he followed me by bike, making sure I got to the right place.

I was already in love with that place!

I entered the one-star hotel Diamond. I had chosen a low priced one, as I still didn't know how long I would be staying. As soon as I entered, I noticed that there was only a dog at the reception desk, which when he saw me, started pissing all over the place.

Immediately the owner came out from the back, took him out and gave me the keys to my room, without me understanding a single word.

I got to a room on the fourth floor that looked like a closet and didn't even have a bed. There was a power socket, a wooden board from wall to wall that formed a sort of coffee table and a kind of sleeping bag, the traditional *futon*. For five pounds a night, it could work.

I put down my suitcases and went to eat in a tiny restaurant on the corner, where there was a screen at the entrance, a photo of the dishes offered and a place to put the money. I looked at about twenty dishes and couldn't figure out what I was ordering, so I pressed one at random and sat down. I couldn't tell exactly what I was eating, but it was all delicious and I just had paid the equivalent of three pounds.

It was Saturday and, after dinner, I began to explore the surrounding area. I headed to the neighbourhood of Namba, which I had read is the centre of Osaka. It was full of flashing bright signs and billboards, which surrounded the most unusual stores, including an inflatable doll store resembling manga characters, which also had a used women's panties dispenser that particularly impressed me.

After a short mini-tour and after getting lost one more time, I sat on a block of marble. Everyone was walking fast, without giving me so much as a glance. I noticed a European looking guy sitting a few meters away from me and started talking to him.

His name was Juan, he was from Malaga and had been in Japan for six months. He was washing dishes in a restaurant while he was studying the language. He was particularly sociable and probably also happy to talk to another European, since we didn't see many of them there.

"I'll take you to a cool place, *vámonos*!"

We walked to a gaijin bar called *Casa Lapichu*, run by a Peruvian who had married a local woman. He had explained to me that in Japan there were, unofficially, two types of bars: the ordinary ones and those for foreigners, the “gaijin bars”, where all the expats or Japanese who wanted to meet foreigners could be found.

There were people from all over the world and a relaxed

atmosphere, a healthy cheerfulness with no hassle. It was really good. I met an Indian engineer, a computer programmer from Dubai and a French chef.

And then I met Yuko. She was a local girl, very simple and friendly, who laughed a lot. She had lived in New York for three years, so she spoke an understandable level of English. She was older than me, she must have been about thirty-seven or so, even though she didn't look like it. We started talking about this and that and exchanged phone numbers.

The next day, she invited me to dinner at her house, located in a small provincial village called Goido, forty minutes from Nara.

It was a very small town, you could have counted five thousand inhabitants overlooking four main streets, with terraced houses, decorated with the traditional pointed roof.

There was also a small convenience store, a bakery selling wonderful cakes and rice paddies that separated the various streets, with street lamps powered by long wavy wires that also connected to the surrounding houses. The landscape perfectly reflected the anime we grew up with!

The local people stared at me as if I was an alien, but also with a fair amount of interest. I arrived at Yuko's house and was surprised that her mother was there too. She was just as kind and cooked the grandest dinner.

Later on, they took me to drink at an Izakaya, where I got wasted on sake, so, given my condition, they offered me to stay for the night. I woke up the next morning alone at their home, with breakfast on the table and a note:

"We are at work and will be back around five, make yourself at home, these are the keys. If you want to stay tonight too, you are welcome, we are happy to have you with us!"

Crazy, I couldn't believe my eyes. I found myself alone in an unknown house, in a remote Japanese suburb, with a fridge and a heart full of good things. Absurdly, I felt more at home there than in London. I was fine there, so I decided to go get my stuff from my depressive closet at the Diamond Hotel and take it to Yuko's house.

I felt indebted, so in the meantime, I went shopping and

prepared dinner for her and her mother, who were pleasantly surprised. After all, a dish of pasta always brings people together, especially when cooked by an Italian!

After dinner, Yuko and I went for a walk in a park nearby.

"How are you so trusting? To leave a stranger in your house?"

"You immediately seemed like a good person to me, I never had any doubts. Besides, there isn't much to steal in my house!"

"Well…Thank you, so much, it was one of the most beautiful gestures I have ever received. May I ask where your father is?"

"He is no longer with us. He decided to end his life a few years ago".

She told me that there was a bad story of money behind it, that her father had not been able to pay back his brother-in-law and so, out of shame, he drove his car off an overpass, trying to get his family the insurance money, which, however, without him knowing, did not cover suicides.

She added that she had never told anyone about it, also because no one had ever even asked her. In Japan it was considered taboo to discuss this type of situation and there was a stigma surrounding it.

But I, with my usual impudence, had had her tell me everything and she was happy to share her pain.

I also told her my story, how lost and confused I felt and how I didn't even know where my mother was.

"Come with me to the Kyoto temple on Saturday. There is an old master there who can perhaps help you find a way".

I was a little dubious about it, but I decided to go with the flow.

After an hour by train, we arrived in one of what was considered the pearl of Japanese tradition. The town of Kyoto stretched out on a straight road that led to the hill of temples, on which dozens of them rose majestically.

We walked to the most imposing and decorated one, where a Buddhist ceremony began shortly afterwards, with the priest ringing a bell, burning incense and meditating, following the words of the old master. I didn't understand anything, but I enjoyed the folkloristic context and the peaceful atmosphere.

The ceremony lasted one hour, after which Yuko took me before the elder. He obviously did not speak English, so she was my interpreter.

"Elder Master Arayama, it is a pleasure to see you again. This is Oliver-San, he came from afar to talk to you. He needs your help."

He stared at me impassively and beckoned me to come closer.

A little awkward, I sat down next to him. He was intimidating.

"Close your eyes and meditate with me, boy."

"...I've never done that, but...okay..."

At first, I felt like an idiot, then after a few minutes I managed to let go. I cleared my mind and felt an energy growing inside me. The old man opened his eyes and put his hand on my forehead.

What you are looking for is not here. And it is not now. Find peace with yourself. Continue to struggle with courage and the universe will present itself to you when the time comes. I see much light in your future. Do not lose hope".

He took his hand off my forehead and accentuated a sort of half smile.

"...Yes but...what does that mean in concrete terms...?", I asked Yuko.

"That you must have patience, stop judging yourself, stop thinking so rationally, continue to follow your authentic path and you will find your way".

"Yes okay... They are beautiful words and very touching, rich in meaning and spirituality... But where do I start? What should I do? I no longer know where my home is, nor what I am supposed to do with my life".

Master Arayuma intervened again:

"Stop when you are tired. Listen to yourself. Take care of yourself. Forgive yourself. Do not bury your emotions, your guilt, your frustrations, your dreams, which you have suppressed because you think they are too big for you or too hard to reach. Stay with yourself, feel your emotions, your pain, your will that you have repressed because life has led you to do so. And when you do not have an answer, stop there and wait. It will come to you from within yourself when you are ready to receive it".

Those words were a little confusing, but they were touching. Maybe I was really too rational to fully understand them, but I decided to trust them and see what would happen. In any case, I had no better alternative. Besides, they say that people who have faith in something are generally happier and improve their chances of personal fulfilment.

I bowed, thanking and greeting the old master and walked with Yuko towards the centre of the city. We were already beginning to catch a glimpse of the famous "Sakura", the first cherry blossoms, which surrounded the traditional temples and the banks of the river, painting a magnificent spectacle. I saw Yuko's protective gaze and her affectionate smile and embraced her.

I was beginning to understand something of what the old man had told me. For example, that moment was perfect as it was. A small moment of happiness.

14.

That trip in Japan was my first trip alone, which allowed me to get out of my shell to see what was out there and I will always cherish a wonderful memory of it.

I decided that, from that moment on, if I found myself undecided in front of a crazy choice, I would jump in and the world would do the rest.

I spent two memorable weeks with Yuko, but the day of my departure inevitably came. We didn't waste much time in the usual small talk. We both knew that, most likely, we would never see each other again and that was fine. Many people come into our lives, some to stay and some at the right time, and that's the way it had been for us.

I greeted her mother warmly and held Yuko in a long hug.

"Sayonara Oliver-san. I hope you'll find your happiness.

Take care of yourself".

"Goodbye Yuko-chan. It was nice to meet you. Take care and keep on brightening the world with your kindness, you're wonderful!"

She smiled at me sweetly and, with her eyes a bit teary, she left, while I walked towards the airport, feeling a mixture of sadness and joy.

I returned to London with a different spirit, more positive and less impatient, keeping in mind the words of the old master. In fact, just a week later, I immediately found a job. Or rather, one of my roommates introduced me to his boss, but it is always a matter of being there, even with the right mindset, at the right time.

I started working as a night receptionist in a hotel in Trafalgar Square, the centre of London, for the most famous hotel chain in the world. It was a rather relaxed job; after midnight I generally had almost nothing to do until seven in the morning.

There were three of us, and my manager was a very easy-going, chubby Indian guy who was also quite comical.

He told me that he had once stretched out sunbathing in a meadow near the woods and had taken off his shirt; but he was so hairy that he risked being shot by hunters, who from afar, mistook him for a wild boar.

He was only four years older than me and we soon became good friends, between cigarettes, food stolen from the kitchen and various misadventures. The latter, above all, was never lacking.

I never thought that working in a hotel would expose you to a multitude of such extravagant situations, many of them bordering on the absurd.

I received every possible kind of complaint: the rooms were too small, the mattress was too hard, the pillow was too soft, the Scottish whisky from 1984 was missing in our bar, the scent of the soaps was too industrial, the view from the room did not overlook the Thames (situated five kilometres further away), there is a ghost in my room and many other fantastic stories. I began to hate people.

Once, an American guest came to tell me that his curtains were too blue, electric blue and that they stopped him from sleeping well.

"So, excuse me, what do you want me to do?"

"It's not my problem, you are in charge of solving problems, so do something."

"The only problem I see here is mental."

"...How dare you...?!! I'll have you fired!"

Fortunately, my manager intervened to moderate the situation and sent me back inside.

I would have kicked him in the ass and dragged him out, that would have been my solution. Of course, he just wanted a discount, like most others.

Anyway, the strategic location of the hotel and its brand also gave us some epic scenes, which can only happen at night in the centre of London.

One evening, our hotel hosted a big event, the corporate party of a famous private employment agency. I remember this little blonde girl, she must have been about twenty-five years old. She got so drunk that she threw up and at the same time shit her pants while sitting on the sofa in the bar. I just complimented her and walked her to her room.

In addition, I was also in charge of room service and even there were "interesting" situations.

I was once bringing a bottle of Champagne to room 412 and walking around the fourth floor.

“AAAAAAAAAAAAAAAAAAAAAHHHHHHH!!!!!!!”

I heard a threatening scream coming from room 409 nearby. I got scared and knocked over the tray, with the bottle falling to the floor. I knocked on her door to see if she was all right, but there was no answer, so I decided to use my master key and entered the room. I saw a man sitting on the toilet gritting his teeth and sweating cold, who looked at me with an air of surprise.

"Are you all right, sir? I heard screaming and I got worried..."
"I'VE GOT HAEMORRHOIDS!! NOW GET THE FUCK OUT, YOU LITTLE SHIT!"

I listened and I swooped out, while he kept yelling, wrestling with *his* shit.

Nevertheless, from time to time, there were also pleasant people to talk to. I definitely remember Emma, a famous writer, or at least quite well known, who was our regular guest in the past four months. She was a beautiful woman in her forties, blonde, tall and shapely. She ordered a glass of red wine every evening and never spared a greeting and a chat. I was surprised by her kindness and humility, normally they would open the door and almost cursed at me as if I was disturbing them, even though they had placed the order themselves. But not her, I was always happy to serve her. One evening she ordered two glasses of red wine.

"Good evening Mrs Emma! Are you expecting someone tonight or has the day been particularly hard?"

"Hi Oliver, the second one is for you. You're the only person keeping me company these days and I wanted to buy you a drink."

Luckily, I wasn't very busy that night, so, although a little hesitant, I decided to accept. She was an extremely sensitive woman and always had something interesting to say on any subject. Emma was particularly beautiful that evening, she wore a long, semi-transparent blue dress that showed off her explosive shape. During our conversation, she confessed to me that she was married to a businessman, who hardly spoke to her anymore. They still shared the same house in Newcastle, in the north of England, but they practically both lived in hotels.

"Too bad for him. You are a fascinating and interesting woman, who would make every day special. I'm sure you'll have a line of admirers."

It was the only banality I was able to say at that moment, feeling rather pathetic and accommodating; but she smiled at me.

"Do you find me attractive?"

"...I do...", I replied a bit embarrassed.

"Come here", she winked. She wrapped herself around my neck and started to kiss me. She took my hands and put them under her dress. She had enormous breasts and she wasn't wearing any underwear. Then she gently dragged me onto the bed and unzipped my trousers. She lifted her dress and we started to do it. In the meantime, I received a call from another room:

"Yes, it's room 318, I'd like to order a club sandwich and a glass of Merlot."

"…Ah…"

" Did you understand me...?"

"Of course sir! There's a bit of a queue in the orders at the moment, but we'll try to do it as soon as possible!"

"Are you sure? Why are you out of breath and there's a woman panting in the background?!"

"...No sir, it's just that I'm very busy with orders and there's a guest who's not feeling well in the room next door!"

"...Ah...yes, yes, yes, I understand...please wash your hands well before making my sandwich...!"

"Certainly sir!"

In the meantime, Emma let herself go to a groan that probably woke up the whole floor. In my head, I was already imagining the discussion of my dismissal.

"Wow...This is truly a five-star service!", she exclaimed.

I zipped up my pants and went to make the club sandwich.

The most incredible anecdote, however, concerns George. He was the oldest concierge of all, sixty-four years old, he had been working there for almost forty years and was close to retirement.

He was of Ghanaian origin, he moved to London with his family when he was a boy and everyone loved him.

One day he felt sick and was taken to hospital, from which he never came out again. His passing was not made public until the following week, at the request of the family. Moreover, the hotel was big and there were over five hundred employees, so people knew each other mostly by sight, but not personally and the news didn't come out for a while. One morning, Carlos and Eddy, two maintenance workers unaware of everything, went to get their usual coffee and saw him sitting there:

"Hey, George! Long-time no see! Maybe it's time you retired?!"

"Oh yes, definitely...! I don't have much time left...Say hello for me to everyone", he stood up and left the room. Then they joined us at the reception for the morning report.

"Where has George gone?" asked Carlos carelessly.

All of them squinted their eyes, including the director, who was visibly upset and annoyed:

"What are you saying? Is this a topic you can joke about?"

"...No... Eddy and I just saw him in the staff room...!"

"George died a fortnight ago, his funeral was the day before yesterday...!"

Frosty silence fell in the room and on their pale faces. I can say almost with certainty that they were not lying, judging by their expression; moreover, I don't think they had any reason to do so, especially on such a delicate subject. George had come to say his last goodbye to his beloved hotel.

15.

My life was beginning to have a certain semblance of normality. I had been working in that hotel for eight months, the longest job I had ever had until then.

One night I started sending my resume online randomly, taken by boredom. The next day, I was contacted by another hotel in the same chain for an interview and it went incredibly well, so I was hired as a night manager.

Moving from a night porter position to a night manager one, was totally out of the ordinary, these things can only happen in London.

In fact, I initially took the hit. There was no one to hide behind when particularly complex situations arose and I certainly did not have the experience to deal with them. However, somehow, I kept the business going. I decided to adopt the only style of management I knew, that of my previous supervisor.

The employees under me became very loyal, they always covered for me, in all circumstances and I covered for them. There was a family-like atmosphere and it was almost a pleasure to go to work, despite the thousands of problems in that hotel. It was a daily battle that we all fought together and I was on the front line. I liked that feeling of leadership, and the engagement it created with my teammates.

I eventually managed to move into a more dignified home. Finally, a flat of my own. However, the price to pay was the location: of course, I couldn't afford anything lavish and the only one that was within my grasp was in front of London City Airport, to the east, in the Docklands.

The house was a bit outdated, but cosy. I even had the living room, with a sofa that sucked you in from how it was smashed and a curved screen television from 1996, that weighed fifty kilos and had only three channels.

Unfortunately, the idiot architect who had designed it had thought well to place the bedroom right on the side of the

Boarding Pass

Valid for one single journey only

Price as published

Number
C493158

Not for resale • Issued subject to conditions - see over

The Emirates Air Line is operated by Docklands Light Railway Limited (DLR).

This Boarding Pass is issued subject to E[illegible] Air Line's Conditions of Carriage, copies of which are available at tfl.gov.uk/tickets or ask fo[illegible]s at the Emirates Air Line ticket offices in the terminals. The Boarding Pass remains the property of DLR and is not transferable from one customer to another. It must be produced for inspection on each journey whether demanded or not.

5 BBP 12 9 8 7 6 5 4 3 2

airstrip and, as if that wasn't enough, the train, the famous DLR, passed in front of it every ten minutes. Not exactly ideal for someone who works at night, but I was still satisfied. I had a steady job, a house, some good friends and a few girls who always passed by.

I remember that on New Year's Eve I was getting ready to go to work, it was two degrees below zero and a sunset lighting up the sky. I sat watching it with my double espresso in my hand and started thinking. To think that during the year, I had really run to the end and fought like a lion. And there I was, in my crumbling new house with an airport view, wearing my manager suit.

As the sun slowly set, I raised my eyes to the sky.

"Did you see what I'm doing Dad? More than cookies! It's tough down here, I miss you, but I'm very strong, you know?! Keep on following the show, it's only the beginning! Happy New Year, wherever you are".

I tied the knot on my tie, put on my coat and walked towards the railway. That was the end of my year, with a new confidence, self-awareness and a lot of hope in my heart.

My career was taking off and I was pushing myself to the edge, trying to climb higher and higher.

After fourteen months as a night manager, I was hired as a reception manager; in a few years, I became operations manager and finally general manager. I was thirty years old and had been in London for seven years.

I was happy with the results I had achieved and finally began to live a dignified existence. I was earning quite well and I had moved again, this time to the Notting Hill district, where everything had started.

Nevertheless, my life was always hectic and stressful. I was beginning to be tired of the city, the perpetual greyness, the unsavoury food, the several months of rain a year and that frenetic, unhealthy lifestyle.

In addition, almost all the friends I had made, had returned home, because London is, for many, just a passing through, an experience of personal growth, which, in the long run, consumes you with its mad pace; there are no idle times like in Italy and everything is constantly changing.

I, on the other hand, had no place to return to. I was down, demotivated and I lived to get to the weekend.

As always, everything came at the right time. While I was busy preparing the report on the projected revenue for the next fifteen months, bored as fuck, I received a phone call from a headhunting agency, which had found my profile online.

"Mr. Oliver Milani? Hello, we would like to offer you a job".

"Ah...What is it?"

"We are looking for a business development manager for the opening of a section of a hotel in Singapore and brand expansion in Southeast Asia, would you be interested?"

Although I wasn't expecting anything else, I felt a little melancholy at the idea of leaving what had become my second home, which had welcomed me with kicks and punches, but always extended a hand to help me get up. All those moments spent in those seven years made their way through my mind: the internship at the Times with Alberto, the shithole with the Polish bricklayers, the first time I was hungry for real, the big nights out, friends and girlfriends from all over the world, who came and went , the beers, the thousand failures, the despair and fear of not making it, and finally, the unexpected joys of conquest, stability and social climbing.

This has been my London, with its adversities, its contradictions and its thousand facets; a city that goes on, always and always, without ever stopping, that gives everyone an opportunity, the chance to always start over and reinvent your own life.

For me, it would remain forever a safe haven to return to; however, it was now the time for a change and to return to looking for my place in the world.

Exactly fifteen days and four interviews later, I found myself sitting in business class, heading for Singapore. The hostess welcomed me with a glass of Champagne and some caviar canapés. I was so thrilled at the idea of my new upcoming experience that I could not sleep much. I watched the entire X-Men filmography, concluding with the Wolverine movie and landed eager to begin my new adventure.

Only from the airport, I began to perceive what kind of reality I had just catapulted myself into. It was totally covered with carpeting, with a bathroom every fifty metres, each one brand new and impeccably clean. Not a thing out of place, everything polished and worked beautifully. I felt almost uncomfortable, but at the same time happy to be part of it.

Forty minutes by subway, or rather known as the MRT (also impeccable) and I found myself in front of the Marina Bay Hotel, what would soon be my new workplace. Three immense asymmetrically shaped towers, with a platform at the top, containing its exclusive infinity pool on the fifty-eighth floor, flanked by the latest bars and restaurants, majestically overlooking the city centre. And down there, there was me, a tiny dot, contemplating that show of lights that illuminated the marina. I sat on a bench in front of me and lit a cigarette, staring at the clear sky, blurred by artificial glow. I felt important. I didn't know how I got there from my little house in the woods where I grew up, nor why.

I had seized life at the right moment and I had taken everything that came with it. Yet something was missing.

Suddenly, a sweet voice interrupted my thoughts:

"Hello!!"

"…Hi…?"

"Are you new here?"

"Yeah, I just got here an hour ago…"

"Ah well...You'd better go and have a smoke back there before a plain-clothes officer fines you five hundred dollars!

"Ah...thanks for the tip! Pleased to meet you, I'm Oliver"

"Jam. Welcome to Singapore!"

"Is your name really jam or is it a nickname?"

"It’s my name! And it's not about food. My mother told me that she met my father in the traffic of Manila, in its usual traffic jam. He hit her car. And from there he decided my name. It's not exactly the most exciting story in the world!"

“Haha sorry but I have to agree! Well, anyway, you are

officially the first person I have talked to in Singapore, apart from the immigration police officer. So, let me buy you a drink!"

"Thank you! I accept gladly!!"

Soon afterwards I understood the reason for her enthusiasm. I initially believed she thought I was cool, in reality, it was because a simple small beer in Singapore cost over seven pounds.

We exchanged small talk for a while. She was a really nice person to talk to and also very curious about me, so I told her more or less my story. She followed me with interest, without ever getting too intrusive with her opinions or disclosing anything about her, but I didn't care.

I wanted to get to know her little by little and I didn't want to be influenced by the label with which our profession normally classifies us. Usually, it is always one of the first questions when two people meet each other. One tends to identify the other by their job and give a hasty judgment, then maybe, like me, you don't even know how you ended up in certain contexts, even though you still have to make a living; even though I found out shortly afterwards that this was definitely not her case.

Jam was born in Singapore but had Filipino/Chinese origins. She was a smart little girl, almond-shaped eyes with a lively look, dark complexion, just over five feet tall and with a very small build; she was thirty-seven years old, but she looked at least ten years younger.

"Wow, what an intense life! I am very pleased to meet you. Now I have to go to another bar, I have an important appointment. Do you want to come too?"

"Well...I don't have any plans and I'm jet-lagged, so I'll gladly accept if you don't mind".

"No problem. You'll see that you'll have fun, there's a special event tonight, but I'm not anticipating anything!"

I already liked Singapore. I had arrived a few hours ago and I was already out and about.

After our drink, she called a cab and took me to the vibrant Clarke Quay area, the centre of the city's nightlife.

When we arrived, everyone started to greet her on the street.

I was confused.

"You are popular in this neighbourhood!"

“Haha! Let's just say, I am at home!"

We walked for about twenty minutes along an illuminated canal full of boats, in a street completely decorated with psychedelic lights and crowded pubs.

We stopped at *The Pink Blues*, where there was an endless crowd at the entrance. I've always hated crowds, especially in bars.

"Sounds nice, but don't you think there are a bit too many people? I was thinking of having a quiet beer"

"Haha! You’re such a country boy! Don't worry, you can come with me, you don't have to stand in line!"

I was getting more and more confused and she seemed amused.

"...Can you explain it to me...?"

"Yes, this place is mine and tonight I am playing here with my band"

"Ah...interesting...!", was the only words that I was able to say, still amazed by the whole situation.

Security made us pass in front of it and I found myself in the backstage.

"Ok I'm going to change, wait for me at table twenty-four, it's reserved for me. Order whatever you want".

Without asking too many questions I went to table twenty-four and ordered a couple of beers.

About twenty minutes later, I saw her come out in a very short and shiny silver dress, with heels of at least six inches. She was welcomed by a warm applause from the whole audience and shortly afterwards she started singing. The first song was in Chinese, but I could appreciate her skills, she was really good and pleasant to listen to.

Her mini-concert went on for about an hour, while I was still pouring beer and I was already a little tipsy. It was almost two in the morning and most of the people had left. Suddenly, she came towards me and dragged me on stage.

"Thank you for coming tonight! Let's end the evening with *Wonderwall* by *Oasis*, in collaboration with a special guest, coming directly from England!"

"...Are you crazy...?! I'm tone deaf!"

“Haha! Relax, we are among friends!"

Embarrassed and tipsy, I picked up the microphone and started singing with her. Or rather shouting into the microphone. I screamed so loud that the floors trembled, but the few customers left seemed to appreciate it, perhaps out of compassion. I didn’t give a damn and decided to have a good time, and I also got a final applause, including from Jam.

It was an epic evening and it was only my first day!

I thanked Jam and walked back to my hotel drunk, which was located in Tanjong Pagar, a half hour walk from Clarke Quay.

In that time, I started thinking about many things. I hadn't yet realised where I was and what I was doing there on the other side of the world, but at that very moment, I was happy; about myself and the situation I had jumped into without hesitation. Afterall, the secret is just this, so trivial, but complex to put into practice at the same time. They told us and repeated it a million times: to enjoy and live in the moment, the famous here and now; for the thousands of problems and worries that constantly grip our brain, there will still be time to think about them tomorrow.

In fact, the next day, all the shit that I did not consider the night before, showed up directly and literally at the door.

"Knock-knock!"

“Um...I only know one person in this country that I met less than 24 hours ago, and I doubt it's her at my door, so...Who the hell is it going to be...?”

I put on a T-shirt and went to open it. He was a big, muscular man, dressed in a suit and tie, with a pit-bull look and a pissed off face.

"…Yes...How can I help you...?"

"Hello, Oliver. My name is Wesley and I am your new boss. I tried to call you, but your cell phone is off and I wanted to have a chat with you."

But what the hell was this at...Eleven in the morning!?

Damn, those blackout curtains were really effective.

"...Ah...Pleasure to meet you!"

I must have a really stupid face.

"Yes, yes, get dressed, I'll wait for you in the lobby bar."

I put on the first things I found and tried to fix my hair, without much success, and went downstairs.

Wesley was sitting on the sofa with a steaming cup of americano and the same menacing look of a few minutes earlier.

"Good morning again, sorry for the delay. Between the tiredness, for the flight and the jet-lag, I didn't hear the alarm clock. It happens to me very rarely."

"Welcome Oliver, I noticed that you have already settled in well", he replied sarcastically.

"In what sense?"

"What did you do last night?"

"Well...Nothing much...I went out for a beer and went back to the hotel..."

"A beer you say..."

"Uhm...yes...maybe two..."

"You see, Singapore is a much smaller place than the big cities we come from and when there is a local celebrity involved, the rumours run very fast."

Then he showed me his cell phone, playing the video of me "singing" *Wonderwall* with a pint in my hand and in an obvious state of drunkenness.

"OH FUCK...!! That is to say...damn it...! I'm sorry, I didn't even know that Jam was so well known, I met her at Marina Bay..."

"Yeah, I know, Jam Wei is a very popular singer in Singapore and she came to open our new club. As you have been chosen and represent one of the pillars of Marina Bay's management, please behave in a manner appropriate to your role, so as not to damage the image of the most influential company in the country. I hope I have explained myself."

"Message received."

"Good. Take a shower and join me, I'll be waiting for you in an hour at Marina Bay to discuss what to do with the rest of the management team".

He got up without even looking me in the face and left. Perfect! As usual, I made a great first impression!

I got my shit together and headed to Marina Bay. It was even more immense than you could perceive from afar.

It had at least twenty entrances, divided between three connected buildings and an endless shopping centre that expanded over four floors. I went to the ground floor, the one reserved for employees. There were turnstiles and security guards to enter.

I had heard that there were over fifteen thousand people working there and probably, the only way to keep order, was to have rules and strict organisation.

I got lost at least twenty times in the first ten minutes.

There were three restaurants dedicated only to the staff, where there were six tables organised in a buffet-style, where there was food of every kind and every cuisine, from local to western, ending with Indian, vegan and halal for the Muslims, who even had dedicated trays of different colours, so as not to risk "contaminating" their dishes with "profane" food. The staff, in fact, came from all over the world and tried in some way to please everyone.

Luckily, I met Marvin, a nice bald Hungarian guy in his forties, who I discovered to be my future colleague and immediately became my guide, starting from the locker rooms. There were three of them, huge and in impeccable condition, with lockers, benches, showers and everything necessary. I saw a couple of people sleeping on the benches.

He explained to me that salaries there were totally variable and could differ greatly even between employees who held the same role, depending on their curriculum and how much they were considered useful by the company.

"So? What's that got to do with it?"

"You see, we are lucky that the company pays for our house, but most of them here are simple employees; many of them are from Malaysia and don't earn enough to afford a room in Singapore, so they travel daily from the nearest neighbouring city, Johor Bahru. Three hours by bus to go, twelve hours of work and another three hours to get home. Sometimes, some people can't make it and they stay over."

That story impressed me a lot, it was pure madness. Actually, when I thought about it, when I lived in Rome it took me almost the same time sometimes, and that was without having to go to another country.

We then went up to the fifty-eighth floor, where we had an appointment with Wesley and the others. To get there we had to take three elevators, it took us almost ten minutes. At the top, we were able to admire a sensational sight: the exclusive infinity pool that stretched around the entire perimeter, with a view of the whole of Singapore on one side and the illuminations of Garden Bay on the other, one of the largest natural parks in the city.

Waiting for us there was the whole team; for that project alone, there would have been a hundred people and I was one of the six managers who managed it. I tried to maintain a serious and dignified attitude, at least at the beginning.

Wesley announced me to the team of employees, who when

they saw me pass, they lowered their heads and waved shyly, almost bowed:

"Hello, boss! Nice to meet you!"

"Thanks, guys, there's no need, keep your heads up and call me Oliver. If you need anything, even if you think it's stupid, I'm always at your disposal".

They seemed almost surprised by my attitude. And I was surprised by such a welcome. I also noticed a look of contempt towards me from a couple of other managers, especially a sour-faced blonde.

We started a preliminary meeting, where we discussed market strategies, concept and timing. What a drag. I have always been a person of action more than a planner. Every time I planned something, the best solution always came to me on the spot.

I got out of there at nine in the evening and it was only the first day. I didn't have a good feeling about this new job, and I didn't care much about what I was doing.

My feelings proved me right as the days went by. I was

working from early morning to late evening and I didn't have time for anything else, not even to think.

I was like in limbo, a seemingly perfect bubble, in which everything was impeccable, because it was designed to be, but there was no trace of emotion.

The city itself transmitted no vibration, negative or positive. Everything was neat, shining and tidy, there were no drugged-up lunatics talking to themselves or screaming for no reason, there were no bums on the street, no jobless people. Was it not, after all, what I had always dreamed of? A civilised place, to be at peace? Maybe. And yet, I kept feeling that there was something missing inside me that I could not explain.

I went out with Marvin on Sunday evening, our only day off. We met on a bench in the garden of my apartment building, where he showed up with a bottle of whiskey and a pack of ice. I smiled as I saw his bald head in the distance, I felt like I was at home. I didn't give a damn about drinking fine cocktails in exclusive clubs, with music and a view of the city. I much preferred to sit in a quiet place with a good friend, the right bottle, a few cigarettes and a genuine conversation.

"Marvin, what are you doing in Singapore?"

"I don't know. I grew up in Hungary, but my brother is one of the most important mobsters in Budapest, so I left when I was sixteen and started my journey around the world. I lived in America, Canada, Mexico, England, Cyprus, Malta, England and finally, I ended up here".

"Wow...what about your family?"

"I left my wife and kids in Manchester. Let's see how things stand here. Also, it is full of beautiful girls, it's a paradise here! There is no hurry!"

"Haha! Be good, you'll end up in your underwear under the bridge!"

We poured ourselves another glass of whiskey and I told him a little bit about my life.

"And you Oliver, how did you end up here?"

"I don't know, I'm beginning to wonder. I spent many years in London and I was tired and demotivated by that kind of life. Actually, I don't know if this one is better."

"Do you like your job?"

"No. I don't even know how it happened to me. The problem is that I never chose it. I took what came in and brought out the best in it."

"I'd say maybe you've hit the nail on the head. You gave up what you liked because inside you felt, maybe, it was too hard to reach or you didn't feel up to it. I speak from experience. I wanted to be a pilot. Between one excuse and another that I was telling myself, I started working in restaurants and today I am here. I am the best at what I do, but...every time I look up and see a plane, I feel a little melancholic."

"You are right. Actually, I've never completely abandoned the idea; I've just put it aside temporarily and I'm sure the right time will come."

" And what would be your goal?"

"I want to write for a living. I've never stopped doing it, even in these years, nor have I ever stopped trying under the radar. I'm just tired of waiting."

"As trivial as it may seem...Enjoy the trip, without being impatient. It is the most beautiful part, which will give you a full life. Every moment of life leaves you with something. Imagine those who do the same job for fifty years and then think about us. And maybe they are also happy like that, there is nothing wrong with that. But think, how many lives have we lived compared to them? If I died tomorrow, I would still be satisfied with what I did. My life has been a great adventure!"

"If you die tomorrow, at forty? Come on, pass me another glass, Indiana Jones!"

"Haha! What an asshole! You've become harsh and insensitive yourself! Don't drink too much or else you'll collapse on the bench like a pussy!"

Actually, my head was starting to spin. He was guzzling whiskey like juice; it was hard to keep up with him.

We drained another glass and went home. I really enjoyed spending it with him and somehow it had partially sedated my sense of uneasiness. In the end, we are all in the same boat, there are only those who believe more, those who do not believe enough and those who, for various reasons, no longer believe.

16.

I had been in Singapore for two months now and I had seen very little, besides the hotel where I worked and my bed.

I took a cold shower to wake up and put on my tailored suit, ready for another day of "passion" in the humid and sultry heat of the city. At the beginning I was sweating even when I was standing still, then, after the first weeks, I got used to the tropical climate.

My new apartment was located in Outram Park, in a condominium on the 22nd floor, part of the historic Pearl Bank complex, which stood on a hill and a large garden in one of the most central areas of the city. I had the subway station right under my house, which meant a ten-minute walk. Everything in Singapore was bigger, especially wider; when I saw something in the distance, it seemed close, but then you had to walk at least another twenty minutes to get there. My neighbourhood was practically attached to Chinatown, one of the most traditional places in the city, full of temples, stalls selling all kinds of mystical objects, restaurants with various typical specialties (including frog porridge, which I never dared to try) and semi-private clubs, where men could go to play pool and have fun with the girls in the evening; or, at least, that's what I heard.

I was early that morning, so I went to the Hindu temple, not far from there, and, for the first time in my life, without thinking too much about it, I closed my eyes and started praying to the four-armed elephant that dominated the hall.

"Dear mystical mega-elephant, give me a sense of direction and help me find the right way. Give me a hand, you who have four! Amen."

I think that was the most foolish prayer he had ever heard. And yet, thinking back on it today, maybe he really did give me a hand.

Shortly afterwards, I went to one of the famous food courts, the food markets which included multiple counters that each served a different specialty for four or five Singapore dollars, about three pounds. The menu for my breakfast was white rice, roast duck slices and hot sauce, with lukewarm sweet coconut milk coffee. Forget about cappuccino and croissants! A hit to the stomach that sends you directly to the bathroom just as you finish.

After a healthy breakfast, I got to work. First, I made sure that the reception and the public areas were in order, although I had no doubts. Everything was going perfectly at Marina Bay, as always, everyone was working like robots.

Finally, I went to check how the opening of the restaurant on the top floor was going. The staff were already assembling everything. Suddenly, a shrill and annoying voice interrupted the harmony:

"What the hell are you doing? You have been on those tables for half an hour! Are you even able to put two tablecloths adequately? Do you need a degree? You are a bunch of idiots! It seems to me that someone is going home today!!"

She was the little blondie with the sour-face, I think her name was Lauren. She had been promoted to supervisor of the restaurant, kissing asses left and right, and maybe she even did something a little extra to get to the top.

I was still one of the people in charge of the whole project and I could definitely have a say. Those poor waiters, who, in my opinion, always gave their souls to their work, were intimidated by her words and started running up and down with their grim and sad eyes. I never put up with those who take it out on the weakest, giving free insults and abusing their position. They were people who sweated their butts off every day for very little money, traveling six hours and working twelve, just to make a living, and many of them also have large families to support. She stood there shouting at them for two tablecloths, to assert her authority and to feel like she's the boss.

Generally, I don't like to brag, exploit my role or make a scene, but that day something snapped inside me, awakening the dormant brawler that was in me:

“Hey blondie... Listen to me... Don't you ever talk to my staff like that again! They are doing an excellent job, we are ahead with the project and you are ruining the professional environment, with direct consequences to the service. The next time I catch you talking like that, it will be you who ends up at home, do you understand?"

She turned at me, surprised, with her eyes wide open:

"...And what do you want? This is my department, so stay in your place! I know what I'm doing!"

I approached her slowly and stared straight into her eyes:

"Perhaps you didn't understand well. I am responsible here for the performance of all departments of the project and you, with your haughty attitude and your unnecessary arrogance, are negatively influencing the performance of the restaurant, compromising the mood of the staff, who are not in the ideal position to provide the best service to customers. But if you would rather, we can discuss this at the table with Wesley and the human resources manager, I am available at all times...And don't you ever dare to answer me or any other member of staff in this way again.

This is the second warning in less than a minute and also the last. Am I clear now?"

She stared at me furiously, bit her tongue and went back to work, with a much better tone of voice. The waiters, who had witnessed the scene, had their faces lit up with satisfaction. Some of them had confided to me that it had been going on for over a month and that she was turning the restaurant into hell, but no one had the courage to speak up for the fear of being fired.

I had just become a god in their eyes, filled with gratitude and admiration. I showed a half smile of satisfaction and everyone smiled back at me. Those were the favourite moments of my job. To be appreciated as a human being, for me it was worth much more than the respect due to the title written on the badge. And, in any case, that bitch really deserved it, even though I knew I had started a cold war.

The next day I had an appointment with Wesley in his office. As I walked down the aisles, there were employees looking down on me and managers pretending not to see me, turning their heads the other way. I didn't care and walked in.

"Oliver, I heard there was some friction between you and Lauren in front of the staff. Before taking action, I would like to know your version."

I told him the facts very precisely.

"I understand the goodness of your intent, however, they are discussions that must not take place in front of the staff. You have humiliated their supervisor, who has lost credibility".

"From my point of view, she has never had any; if the only way a manager has to be respected is to subdue and verbally abuse her staff, she is not up to her task and from this position I am adamant. As I told her already, doing so compromises the mood of the staff and only damages the level of service".

"I appreciate your point of view, but you have been hired to lead the project finance and not from an operational point of view. I don't want to see you interact with the restaurant, the reception, the public area and so on. If there is any problem, come and report it directly back to me".

"If that's all you can say, Wesley, I'm not going to work for someone who doesn't know how to respect their team. We are nothing without them. It is such a trivial obviousness that I never imagined I would have to discuss it here with you, the Director of Singapore's Marina Bay."

"Well. I take note of your decision. Only a fool would give up such an opportunity so easily, but it seems that you have already made your choice."

"It's been a pleasure. Good luck."

I returned my things and left. After just two months, my adventure at Marina Bay had already ended. I was glad to have been a part of it and, at the same time, to be away from that toxic and unhealthy environment.

I decided to take some time for myself. After all, I had been running for years without ever stopping and I needed a break.

I started going out every night with different girls. In Asia, I was definitely popular, more than any other place I had been.

Out of all of them, there was one that stuck in my memory. Her name was Glynn, she had oriental features, a South American silhouette and she was a few years older than me. I met her in a bar on Clarke Quay's river. Her husband was a businessman, often traveling around the world, so she had a lot of free time, like me.

One night, we found ourselves on the rocks of the East Coast, a vast stretch of beach in a park that stretched for about six miles, surrounded by palm trees and a bike path. It was not the main beach of the city, many preferred to go to the island of Sentosa, where there was one artificially created for bathing and tourists.

After spending the day at the beach, tanning, chatting and drinking beer, we decided to stop there to watch the sunset and we found ourselves alone on the beach.

There were at least a hundred ships on the horizon and a faint shade of pink that accompanied the sunset. We could also see the lights of Batam, a nearby island belonging to Indonesia. While I was enjoying the picturesque scenery, Glynn climbed into my arms and began to kiss me gently on the neck. Then she spread her legs, moved her bathing suit on the side and we started to do it, while the sun went down and the waves cradled us. We risked going to jail, but there and then the attraction was too strong. It was definitely memorable.

We had dinner shortly afterwards in a food court nearby, where they only served fresh grilled fish and seafood. She stared at me smugly as I tried to skin a shrimp. I must have looked very similar to Mr Bean, but she didn't seem to mind. Nor did it matter to me. I felt good with her, but I was not emotionally involved. After all, I had never been actually involved with anyone, even if there was a lot of empathy with her.

After dinner, in which I ate almost nothing because of the difficulty in removing the bones and skinning the shellfish, we sat on the rocks and opened another beer.

"Glynn, are you happy with your life?"

"No one has ever asked me that…Hell I have never asked myself that. I don't know how to give a precise answer. Let's say it's okay."

I was silent and she paused, staring at the ships on the horizon.

"I'd like to sail on one of those ships and never come back."

"So...Maybe you're not so happy about it."

"Maybe not. But not everyone is resourceful like you and you are nobody to judge me. I have my life, my things, my certainties. I too dreamt of Prince Charming and a large family. I got married at the age of twenty-two, dazzled by the apparent love of my husband who took care of me. I came from a very poor family and it seemed like salvation, the long-awaited social redemption. And I had it. Just like an emptiness inside that never went away, unlike my husband, who shows up at home twice a month to empty his suitcase and leave again. Everyone dreams of a full and happy life, but the truth is that there always comes a time when you have to distinguish the dream from reality and make the best out of your situation".

I observed her gaze filled with resignation, a woman who had swallowed and repressed her feelings all her life, seeing in her eyes that unexpressed and genuine love that she had dreamed so much of and had never materialised.

I hugged her without answering anything, also because I did not know what to say. She was too intelligent to be comforted by the usual platitudes.

"And you Oliver, are you happy?"

"I am happy to have met you!"

“Haha! Don't be an idiot! Tell me, with that proud look of yours, are you aware and satisfied with how you are leading your existence?"

"I am not. But I am working on it, I haven't given up yet. And neither should you."

"Have you ever fallen in love?"

"Never. How could I? The first woman in my life has abandoned me. How could I ever trust another woman again?"

"In what way?"

"My mother left when I was seven. Without a logical explanation. As far as I remember, I loved her deeply and she left me there alone with my father. And she never looked for me after all these years. I missed her every day of my life."

"I'm sorry... But you can never know what is really behind things. Each person carries on his or her own battle, which you may have no idea about. Have you ever tried to find her?"

"I have thought about it many times... And then I came to the conclusion that no matter what the reason was, there is no good reason to abandon your child. A part of me would like to meet her again one day, to ask her why, if there is even a reason; on the other side, I will never be ready to do so. Then, maybe, now she has another family, other children more desired than me. These are potential truths that I have no intention of learning about. Let's say that it went the way it went and it's fine".

She looked down, with a look of sorrow on her face and put her head on my shoulder. Another sip of beer and we fell asleep.

17.

Another month went by and I was still out of work, even though I kept sending resumes. I was also bored by my superficial daily nights-out and I was becoming rather impatient.

During one evening, I went to one of those semi-private places mentioned earlier, right on my doorstep. As soon as I entered, I saw the neon lights that sparkled on Marvin's bald spot. There was a Filipino girl, at least twenty years younger than him, sitting on his lap, feeding him peanuts.

"Look at the pig! Are you hungry, poor little beast?!"

"Haha Oliver!!! Let me introduce you to Mariel! She's a very nice girl...!"

"I can see that!"

"So, what about you? Have you found a job?"

"Not yet. I am not very convinced to stay in Singapore."

"Excuse me sweetheart, I would like to have a chat with my friend, I'll be back in a little while", Marvin said to the girl, moving away and approaching me.

"Oliver... Maybe it's not a question of where you are or where you are going... Maybe it's time to decide what you want to do with your life. You're at the top of what you're doing right now, you're number one; if you can't find a job it's also because, deep inside, you don't want it that much. If you still have the strength and courage to believe in what you want, if you have a goal... Go straight for it. Or you will find yourself in your forties like me, with a bland life, but with the regret of what it would have been like if you had really tried".

I lowered my head and stopped to think. He was right. I didn't give a damn about running hotels or being number one in the business. The time had come to find my true path, or at least take it back to where I had left it, out of fear or necessity.

"Thank you, Marvin, you are always inspiring. I will leave

you to your business, which is certainly more interesting!"

"Whenever you want Oliver, it's always a pleasure! Ah, please send me your resume when you get home, I lost mine. You never know, I too may still have a chance!"

"Great! It will be done!"

After the umpteenth week I spent sending some resumes without too much conviction and without an answer, I decided it was time to change my mind and take my life back in my hands. In those days, I had thought long and hard about the conversation with Marvin and I was convinced that he was totally right. I felt I had to change something, even though I still had no idea what to do or how to do it.

I began to wander around on Google Maps for about twenty minutes. I dwelt on an image of a cliff surrounded by nature, overlooking the ocean: it was a photo of the island of Bali, in Indonesia, which was just two and a half hours from Singapore. It seemed like the perfect destination. I was looking for a quiet and cheap place to clear my head, a moment of clarity on how to find a sense of direction; and what better place than the so-called "Island of the Gods"?

I didn't want to wait even one more day. I packed all my things and called a cab, heading to the airport.

I started to have a conversation with the taxi driver. He was a Chinese gentleman, in his sixties, who told me that he had settled in Singapore a few years ago.

"You know kid, in Shanghai, I was the head of a big multinational company. I was earning a lot of money, but I was not happy. And I didn't even realise it, I had no time to think! I worked fourteen hours a day and, even though I owned all kinds of goods, I had nothing really. I threw forty years of my life behind money, without ever having the time to enjoy it. Then my wife left me and took everything I had."

"Wow...that must have been quite a blow."

"It was. But perhaps it is also the only thing that saved me. With what I had left, I started to travel and enjoy everything I had not done until then. I met a woman here and remarried. It was like being born again, waking up from a bad dream".

"Just between us, foreigner to foreigner... I have been in Singapore for three months. Beautiful yes, all clean, bright, perfect. But doesn't it seem to you like a fictitious life? It's as if everything here always goes in one direction, in the only possible one, as if every story has an ending that has already been written. What's special about this city?"

"Well...You see, young man, many times it depends on where you find yourself in your life. Singapore is a great place to settle down, living quietly and carrying on your life, pursuing your goals... If you have any. Otherwise, it remains a safe and clean place to survive, nothing special, without too many twists and turns. But what people find hard to understand is, above all, that Singapore is such a perfect place because of its people. It is they who make it what it is, in every aspect. Maybe you didn't stay long enough to appreciate it deeply, but I am sure that, if one day you come back here, you will understand my words".

I said goodbye to the taxi driver and entered the airport. I looked at my cell phone and saw that it was set to airplane mode, I had probably pressed the button accidentally. When I unlocked it, I started to receive about thirty repeated emails and voice mail notifications. Most of them were sent from various hotels and contained similar content:

"Dear Oliver, we have received your resume and would be interested in discussing it with you personally. Please inform us which date would be more convenient to arrange an interview".

I could not believe it. There was also a message from Marvin:

'Call me, it's urgent.'

I knew that at that hour they still had to open the restaurant for dinner and I video called him immediately, to see if he knew anything about it. He was right there with the rest of the staff behind him:

"Hello, Marvin? What the hell happened? I've received at least twenty emails asking me to attend an interview, from companies I've never even contacted, I don't know if you had anything to do with it, but I can't think of anyone else...".

"Haha! I haven't done anything! I just passed your resume on to the guys back here, who sent over three hundred applications in your name, when they heard that you wanted to leave Singapore!"

I saw in the background the smiling faces of my former colleagues, saying hello and asking me to stay. I was deeply moved, I couldn't say anything.

"...I don't know how to thank you! You are amazing!! Thank you, from the bottom of my heart!! I will soon return to embrace you all!!"

"So, what are you doing Oliver, are you really leaving?!"

"...Yes, Marvin... As you said, it's time to find my purpose in life, this is not my life. I feel pathetic just saying it and I don't know if I'm going to make it, but I have to try. If I fail, I will come back to serve at the tables with you!"

"Bravo Oliver, you have all our support! We will miss you! Have a good trip and keep us updated!"

"Goodbye my friends and thanks for everything! I love you all!"

Before boarding the flight, I turned around to take a last look and I remembered the words of the taxi driver, which I finally understood; he was totally right. Singapore is such a good place because of, more than anything, the people who live there.

18.

Two and a half hours later, I landed at Denpasar Airport. The air was already fresher than the humid and torrid climate of Singapore.

Hundreds of taxi drivers at the exit were trying to grab the tourists who had just landed, attacking them at first sight in their very broken English. Despite the crowd, however, they all seemed very relaxed and cheerful and this immediately made me feel at ease.

I got into Wayan's cab, obviously without a taximeter; a rusty red Toyota Corolla from '99, just like the air freshener hanging on the mirror, giving the smell of rotting corpse inside. I tried not to pay attention to it, observing outside the window a reality unknown and never imagined until then, made of palm trees, strange monuments that stood on street corners and traffic circles, depicting curious humanoid looking figures, between the divine and the mythological. And many scooters whizzing everywhere, right, left, across, with two to five passengers on them. A reality decidedly more open than the strict rules of Singapore, where even chewing gum is illegal.

When I arrived at my destination, the taxi driver helped me carry my suitcases to my doorstep, thanking me almost theatrically and making sure that someone opened the door for me. I had booked a villa in the area of Ubud, surrounded by a vast expanse of green rice fields and a dense forest, known for its tranquillity, where many tourists found refuge and regeneration from the chaos of their daily lives.

One of the advantages of Bali is undoubtedly the cost of living: that dream house with a view and private swimming pool only cost me twelve pounds a day!

I was greeted by a local old lady, who didn't speak English but had a warm smile always on her face. She showed me the house and the services included. It was even better than I had expected. Finally, after years of living in hovels of the worst kind, I could afford to live like a normal person!

The fridge was well stocked with all kinds of drinks. I opened a beer and went to sit on the terrace overlooking the forest. Finally, I was at peace.

But you know, peace amplifies thoughts and so does beer. In the last few years, I had been running like crazy without ever stopping, constantly busy trying to reach a goal which, once conquered, I realised had no value for me.

I had been with hundreds of people, girls and occasional friends, but I had never been with myself. I had built my confidence in what was well judged by others, without ever wondering if it was really what I wanted, the important thing was to get there, then we'll see.

And there I was. I had just turned thirty and I had taken my first step towards the so unoriginal, widespread concept of the pursuit of my happiness. I realised that I had been living life on autopilot, although not without twists and turns, but probably not mine. A passive actor of his own existence, who endured what life had thrown at him, while making the most of the few bricks he had found in his hands, building his shaky hut, with cracks everywhere and poor foundations, which was on the brink of collapsing at the first shock. A circular marathon instead of a straight line, which had not brought me to the finish line, but only exhausted me, by running in the same circle now dug into the earth, deeper and deeper, until it became a trench from where you could no longer see the exit.

I took a selfie with my cell phone and examined my face in depth. Was I the guy on the screen? I could not tell, because I had never looked at myself in depth. I didn't know myself at all. I had become very skilful at being any kind of person, depending on the situation I was in, maintaining some distinctive traits of my personality, also perfectly constructed, so that I could be appreciated and recognised, but I had never met the real Oliver.

So, I made a decision: from that moment on, I would only do what made me happy. No more bullshit, smiles and platitudes, moves made because I MUST: from that moment on, I would do only what I WANTED.

I took a blank sheet of paper and divided it in two: on one

side, I started to write everything I wanted to eliminate from my daily life, including a nice thick line on it and on the other, a list, no matter how absurd, of all the things I wanted to do from that moment on.

After an hour of scribbling and two more beers, the list was drawn up and reduced to three simple entries:

_ TRAVEL AS MUCH AS POSSIBLE: whenever and wherever I wanted to, without any economic or time restrictions. Go anywhere I wanted to, depending on my mood and how I woke up that morning, as I did with Bali: go to the airport, get on the first plane and stay there as long as I felt like it.

_ START WRITING AGAIN: after all, it has always been my true vocation, even though I had to give it up to follow a more "appropriate" social path: it was time to resurrect that hopeful little boy I had buried to survive at the end of my internship in London.

_ BE FREE: mentally, financially. From the pain of my past and worries for the future. Don't do anything that hasn't come from the heart anymore, with the only goal being achieving good results in my career, my social recognition or other futile purposes, which are useless to my personal fulfilment.

This last point, which seemed to me almost utopian even while I was writing it, it slowly began to make more and more sense as a guideline for the path I had chosen to take. Yes, *chosen*: finally, I was beginning to choose how I wanted to set my existence, instead of continuing to suffer its events.

I re-read the list a dozen times before falling asleep. Yes, I really liked it! I tore a piece of tape and stuck it next to the window of my new house with a forest view, definitely the perfect place, which tasted like...freedom.

The next day I woke up at dawn. Although I had fallen asleep very late the night before, I felt energetic. I took the scooter supplied to me, which obviously could have only been a *Honda Bali*, identical to my mythical former scooter, and I started riding, without a precise destination in mind.

I crossed the whole forest of Ubud, riding north for about two hours. The road was increasingly hilly, almost mountainous and the poor moped, already a bit shabby, was struggling uphill.

Suddenly, a family of angry baboons came out from the sides of the road and began to chase me, for no good reason. It was history repeating itself, like that wild boar fifteen years before: identical hunk of junk scooter, pushed to its limit, for a maximum speed of twenty miles per hour, but in another hemisphere!

I managed to lose the baboons after a couple of bends (or rather, they stopped chasing me) and I started to laugh out loud, thinking back to the absurdity of the analogy and the old days. I liked to think that, probably, my father was laughing somewhere too, watching the scene.

Meanwhile, the climb continued. There were almost no more cars around and I found myself in front of a breath-taking view, with the Batur volcano and its lake bordering it, with lush greenery surrounding it. What a spectacle! I decided to stop for a while on that plateau. I was in no hurry to run anywhere, nor any obligation of any kind. I could enjoy the moment as much as I wanted. And it was a fantastic feeling.

I got back on the road, continuing an increasingly steep climb. The road had become narrower and narrower and there was no traffic at all; you could only see a few traditional houses scattered in the bushes, a few chickens crossing the road and some colourful birds that I've never seen before.

And then…"BOOM"! Suddenly a deafening burst and the scooter broke down. I took out my cell phone in the vague hope that there was a mechanic or something similar maybe not too far from there, but I was in such a remote area that there was no signal.

As they say, when it rains it pours and such a phrase was never more appropriate: in a few minutes, a torrential rain began to come down.

I remained motionless for a couple of minutes, I didn't

know whether to laugh or cry. I parked my scooter and took partial shelter under a tree. I knew it was not recommended, but after all, I thought, after two misfortunes so close to each other, it was statistically unlikely that I would even get struck by lightning, unless it was fate, which in that case I would have accepted with peace of mind.

I stayed under the tree for a good while and, as much as it sheltered me, after twenty minutes I was already soaking wet. I was beginning to wonder when and how I would come out of it that time, when a little boy, who must have been about thirteen years old, came out of a little house a few metres away. He looked at me and beckoned me to join him.

I was a little hesitant, but I had no better ideas at the time. I entered that modest little house, a bit bare yet very tidy, typical of the Balinese villages, with some stone statues of some local god unknown to me at the entrance and a large wooden canopy.

Balinese architecture is very particular and it is based on the Hindu principle of dharma: every object in the universe is designed to have its own ideal position, in which it must remain aligned in order to achieve complete harmony with the universe. Indeed, if I think about the conditions in which my room was generally laid out, perhaps that would explain why my life was always so messed up.

At home, there was a family with two other children, an old lady and a girl who I assumed was his mother. They were all staring at me curiously and, at first, I felt a bit uncomfortable, also because I didn't look my best, with a torn pair of shorts and a totally soaked t-shirt. I introduced myself and tried to break the ice, but none of them spoke English, nor Italian.

However, somehow, we understood each other through gestures and facial expressions. The older woman smiled at me and brought me a towel and a cup of tea, which I gladly accepted. We were looking at each other, waiting for the rain to pass while the children played with toy cars. I don't think I had seen any for twenty years, let alone children playing with them; but then again, there wasn't any signal up there and even the television wasn't working. It was as if, in that little village at the top of the hill, time had stopped.

After half an hour, another guy entered the house, he looked about twenty-seven years old. He looked at me a little surprised, until the old woman explained (or at least, so I imagined) the situation.

"Hi, my name is Wayan! Welcome to our home!"

Wayan spoke English, unlike the rest of the family. I had met two guys since I arrived on the island and they were both named Wayan. We started talking to get to know each other better, while he was translating to the others and they explained to me that in Bali the same names are traditionally used, according to the order in which the children are born: the firstborn is called Wayan, the second Made, the third Nyoman and the fourth Ketut; in case of the fifth child, the round would start again.

He told me that he was originally from that place but grew up on the island of Java and learned English at the University of Jakarta, where he had moved at the age of twenty to study tourism. He then returned to Bali to look job in a hotel, where he met his wife, sitting with the others watching our conversation curiously.

"So young and already married?"

"Haha yes, for five years! And they are my children!"

I was amazed. He explained to me how it was normal for them to get married very young and build a family, also out of economic necessity. Wayan had worked in a hotel for some time, then chose to help his father-in-law with the family business when he started to have health problems and took it on alone when he passed away. He had a stall in a market in Buleleng, the nearest town, where he sold clothes and T-shirts from the soccer teams. That day he had to close everything because of the sudden torrential rain.

"We did not expect it, in this area of Bali it hadn't rained for nine months!"

"I had no doubt!", I answered among the general laughter.

"But it's positive! Our crops needed it, you brought us luck!"

"It pleases me!", I answered sarcastically, while they

continued to laugh.

A warm and festive atmosphere had been created, even though I found myself in a house in the middle of nowhere on the other side of the world, joking with perfect strangers who barely understood me.

"Wayan, so you lived in the city, in the midst of technology and experienced all the modern comforts that come with it. Don't you miss something there? How can you live up here without internet and television?"

"Oliver...", he smiled, "I often ask myself the same question the other way around... How can you live in a place that is constantly overcrowded, where you can't breathe good air, everyone is nervous, tired and unhappy, millions of people confined in one place but locked up in the solitude of their small screen, in a tiny house that they will end up paying for after forty years of a job they don't want to do? I have everything I need to be happy here...my vegetable garden, the hens laying eggs, a paddy field nearby, wholesale clothes, a good company, clean air...And even the *Serie A* at the village bar!"

"The *Serie A*?"

"Sure, the *Serie A* of soccer! Here we love the Italian *Serie A*, I always go to watch it with friends! Who is your favourite player?"

"Unbelievable, I would have never imagined it! Well... Regardless of the team, Cristiano Ronaldo does extraordinary things, I really enjoy seeing him play!"

"He is also my favourite! Wait a second..."

He took the duffel bag with which he had returned and pulled out a Ronaldo jersey.

"Try it on! You need some dry clothes".

"Wow thank you, it's beautiful!"

I asked him how much it cost, but he wouldn't accept money from me.

"You are our guest, this is our keepsake. Keep it with care!"

"I will, I promise!"

Finally, the rain had stopped. As if by magic, the sky was clear again. Now I had the problem of how to get back.

Who knows if it would work, I thought. I approached my helpless *Honda Bali* and, mindful of a similar previous experience, I tried to restart it with the side pedal. One, two, three...ten...Finally, it started again! The poor twenty-year-old moped was only very tired, but still alive.

I thanked Wayan and his family for their thoughtful hospitality and I hit the road again. In about twenty minutes I found myself on the coast of Lovina, in the far north of the island, one of the less touristic areas. I sat in a *warung*, (a typical local bar/restaurant, very modest and incredibly cheap) overlooking the sea, drinking a coffee, enjoying every moment. I sat there thinking, observing, dreaming for a couple of hours, while the sun went down, giving me one of the most beautiful sunsets ever seen.

What a wonderful day. Moments of true happiness. Of pure life.

19.

A light breeze caressed my face as I enjoyed the sound of the waves crashing on Echo Beach, chilling in a bar on a comfy sofa, in the company of a Corona with lime.

It had already been two months since I arrived in Bali.

I had not yet decided what to do with my life, but in the meantime, I was applying the three rules that I had set myself, trying to live every single day to the fullest, depending on what I wanted to do. I had travelled far and wide around the island, without ever having a fixed destination, sometimes finding myself in front of unexpected beauties or totally unexplored areas, always in the company of my scooter.

I had visited the Hindu temple of Uluwatu, one of the most fascinating and ancient on the island, which stood on a high cliff overlooking the ocean, where you could breathe a mystical atmosphere and enjoy a breath-taking view; the terrace of Tegallalang, a hill composed entirely of layers of rice fields and surrounded by jungle, that offered a majestic scenery; the beach of Kuta, overcrowded with nightclubs and Australian surfers, and the beach of Sanur, cleaner and farther from tourists, with a flat sea, coconuts to drink from and kiosks to eat freshly caught tuna and salmon fillets.

Tired of living like a hermit between the jungle and the forest (and tired of insects), I was ready to reunite with civilisation, so I decided to move to the sea, near the Canggu area, livelier and more vibrant than Ubud, and home to many digital nomads from all over the world. It was a concept that had always fascinated me and that I wanted to explore further: to work remotely, from anywhere in the world and at any time, as long as I had a laptop and an internet connection.

I met many of them in the coffee shops of Canggu and I often exchanged a few words, to try and get their secrets.

Also, because, although Bali was very cheap, my savings

were starting to thin out and I had no intention of going back to working in hotels.

The problem was that many of these jobs required specific skills, such as computer engineering or web design, or that it took too long to make satisfactory earnings, such as creating a blog or writing web content, and I had no experience in the field.

One day, after ordering my usual double espresso in the only coffee shop in the area that makes a decent one, I met John, a nice Australian in his fifties who was in charge of legal and financial consulting online. He was a very cheerful man, relaxed and self-confident at the same time. After the usual pleasantries, I asked him to tell me his story.

"I was working in a law firm in Sydney, entering the office at seven in the morning and leaving at eight in the evening, going to waste myself with beer to numb my brain and suppress my dissatisfaction. I hadn't even considered changing my life, on the contrary, it scared the hell out of me and I had it well hidden in some remote corner of my mind; I had studied my whole life to get where I was, with a prestigious position, where I earned a lot of money. What fool would have thrown it all away like that? I hated every second of that life I was living, but I was convinced that that was the only way, because that's the way everyone is: you have to suffer to survive, to be worth something, to get something and be appreciated. Then one night I received a message from a friend and colleague of mine, his name was Henry, we had started working for the studio at the same time and we had been working together for more than twenty years. He told me that he had been diagnosed with cancer and he had a few months to live. Obviously, I was shocked, and even more so by his death, which occurred just two months later. Something clicked in my head there. What if it was me instead of Henry? My life would have been all there, locked inside those four walls, getting stressed and getting drunk so I didn't have to think about it, while I was exchanging my life for the growth of my bank balance. Think, what a pathetic and insignificant life it would have been? That was certainly not the end I wanted to have. Poor Henry made me promise, before he left, not to screw up like him. So, I quit my job and with the savings

I had, I opened an online legal consulting agency, accessible to everyone in terms of price; I work as much as I want, whenever I want and do good for others. And, guess what? I earn even more money than before!"

His story had weighed me down and inspired me at the same time.

"It's a beautiful story and I couldn't agree with you more. But don't you think that if everyone did that, we wouldn't even have the basic goods and services anymore?"

"I don't think so...We would certainly have less of them, scaled to our real need, just as I believe that the world would go much slower. And, maybe, we would all start to focus again on how much value the simplest and most natural things can have, like a walk by the sea, an extra dinner with your father or a coffee with a friend, instead of thinking about increasing the income of someone else who could already enable his future eight generations to live off his wealth!"

"You are absolutely right! Thank you, it was a pleasure to talk to you. And sincerely, I am very intrigued by your lifestyle, but I don't know where to start, nor do I have any particular skills. What would you advise me?"

"Well, I don't know you well enough to be able to suggest what exactly you could do. What I can recommend is to focus on your knowledge and skills, thinking differently, imagining how you could use them. And don't tell me that you don't know how to do anything, everyone knows how to do at least one thing well in their life.

Do you see that girl sitting over there drinking Coke? Her name is Amanda, I've talked to her two or three times, she lives nearby too. She is a total disaster at everything, from A to Z. BUT…She knows how to give great blowjobs! And, you know, she has a YouTube channel where she teaches how to do them. She makes a living ONLY with that!

Now, she is an extreme case, but you, for example, already know two languages, right? While you're researching, studying and preparing for your next move, it might be a good option to support yourself; by doing just three lessons a day, you've already paid for the day in Bali!"

It didn't seem like a bad idea at all. I said goodbye to John and walked home. As soon as I got back, I sat on the balcony and started fiddling around on my laptop, looking for the best sites to teach languages online. I looked at the first five and signed up for all of them.

For my presentation, I created a video with the ocean in the background, showing off my best smile.

An hour after posting it on my profiles, I received over a dozen requests. It was working! My first step towards economic independence started from there.

After a week I already had regular "clients", four Chinese, two Russians and one Thai; five people who wanted to learn English and two Italian. At first, it was harder than expected, having never taught anything in general, let alone a language to people who do not even understand you; I won most of my students due to sympathy and kindness. Then, I gradually organised myself, drawing up a list of lesson plans of varying levels and homework. I was making about a hundred and twenty dollars a week, working three to four hours a day.

Once I got a good number of positive reviews, I received

more and more requests and I was able to increase my fee to as much as fifteen dollars an hour.

After just three weeks, I was now receiving around $300 a week, which was enough for one month's rent in Bali, working an average of three hours a day and then taking the rest of the day for myself. It was certainly not my final goal, but a first small turning point that allowed me to gain more time to understand which direction I wanted to go in, to continue being free from all constraints.

I was happy with this little achievement and that night I decided to go and celebrate.

I jumped on the scooter and started riding around, as always, without a precise destination. I found myself in a small place with soft light, decorated with colourful lanterns, hidden a few meters from the forest; it was a jazz bar playing live music and I decided to go in for a glass or two.

The musicians and singers were incredibly talented and it had a nice atmosphere.

I was sitting at the bar sipping my third glass of whiskey,

when I noticed her sitting a few metres away. She had strikingly exotic oriental features, with very white, smooth and perfect skin, long hair that draped down her naked back and an intense look. She was the most beautiful girl I had ever seen in my life. Normally, I would have moved closer to her, trying to approach her with one of my usual stupid pickup lines from my poor repertoire, but her beauty and perfection intimidated me, leaving me petrified sitting on that stool.

She noticed that I was looking at her. Our eyes crossed for three very long seconds, in which I had already embarked on a mental journey about her in a wedding dress, our children's names and our future dog.

I looked the other way so as not to seem too intrusive and I tried to think of the least stupid way I could introduce myself. In the end, I decided to improvise, as I had always done. I turned around again, determined to get closer and her stool was suddenly empty. She was gone.

A series of various swearwords echoed in my brain. Perhaps she was still around. I began to look around, in every corner of the place. Nothing, there was no trace of her.

Disheartened, I went out for a cigarette and I suddenly saw her, she was standing a few metres away from me.

'Well, this is my chance!', I thought.

I was reminded of the words of an old high school professor of mine, in which he explained that a stranger had a general impression of us within the first seven seconds.

I approached with eagerness, stumbling into the small palm tree located by the door of that place, uprooting it from the pot and ending up on the ground like a fool. Excellent first impression.

"Oh my God, did you hurt yourself?"

She came towards me and helped me to get up.

"Yes, I believe it's serious, I don't think I'll survive the night".

She looked at me for a few seconds before she understood the joke. Then we both burst out laughing.

"Are you waiting for someone?"

"I called a cab, but I think he got lost".

"It happens often, many streets here do not even have a name! Anyway, if you want, I can give you a lift..."

"Wow, you don’t waste any time! Anyway, you are very kind, but I don't accept rides from strangers."

"All right. Then I’ll introduce myself, my name is Oliver."

"I am Ryn"

"Good! Now that we have met, can we go?"

"Haha! Now that I know your name, yes, I can trust you!"

"Eh, but if I tell you everything right away, that’s no fun."

"You are right! Let's do this, if you guess where I come from, I'll think about it…"

"China? Japan? Hong Kong?"

"No"

"A clue?"

"Um...I eat kimchi regularly"

"What the hell is that?"

She laughed. While I was looking for what kimchi was on

my cell phone, her cab arrived.

"It was nice to meet you, Oliver. See you around!"

"No wait! South Korea!"

She smiled and winked at me from the window, before disappearing around the first corner a few metres away. I felt like an asshole. Instead of looking for what kimchi was, I could have asked her for her number. As if it was such a delicacy, it was cabbage leaves fermented in hot sauce.

I thought about her all evening. We had chatted about nothing for just a couple of minutes, yet it had been special; there was an inexplicable complicity in our looks. Or maybe I was just daydreaming. Who knows what she had thought? Maybe she had already forgotten about it. I wanted to get out and go to her, but I didn't know anything else but her name and that she eats kimchi.

I went back to the same place the next night, but she didn't come. I searched the beaches of the neighbouring area in the following days, but there was no trace of her. What a pity. But after all, I knew absolutely nothing about her, maybe she already had a guy waiting for her at home. I was trying to find every possible excuse to stop thinking about her. After all, it was not normal after two minutes of conversation to get so much into someone like that.

'Come on Oliver, what the fuck are you doing, stay focused on your projects. Now that you're doing well, don't get distracted by a girl', I kept repeating, trying to motivate myself.

So, I decided to focus on what I had to do and locked myself indoors for a couple of weeks. I kept growing my savings teaching English and Italian online, while I was studying web marketing and web design. In a few days, I was able to build my first website, which I decided would become a sort of online journal and logbook. Not the usual travel blog, it had to be something unique and sought after.

I started writing one article a day, on the most varied and unlikely topics, talking about secondary news that no one mentioned in the most famous newspapers. For example, I wrote the first article about a guy who gave a sleeping pill to a child on the plane; it was shared several times on various social media, shortly becoming viral, to my surprise.

I knew I still had a long way to go before I established myself, but I did it without any pressure or expectations, just for the sake of writing and creating something of my own.

When I began to get the first hundred visitors, it was a huge satisfaction. I still didn't gain anything, but somehow one of my dreams was taking shape.

Everything, in general, was finally shaping up rather well. Having become a "top teacher" on the various applications, I was getting more requests than I needed to make a living, so I started being more selective with students.

I always had my loyal ones, I discarded the ones who just couldn't make it, and every now and then I'd enrol a few new entries, just to meet new people.

That day I opened my profile to see the daily requests and I was stunned:

"RYN!!"

I couldn't believe my eyes. I checked her profile several

times to make sure it was her. I had no doubt, the angelic face in the profile picture was the same one that had captured me instantly in that bar.

Her message said:

"Hello Oliver! I'm learning Italian, can you help me?"

Wow. I had wide smile on my face. I immediately answered her. Or almost, after rephrasing the message a dozen times. In the end, I opted for a sober and simple:

"Hello, Ryn! How nice to hear from you again. Are you still in Bali? I would be very happy to help you with your Italian. When are you available for the first lesson?"

I was checking my email every five minutes, waiting for a reply. After a couple of hours, I started to think that I was being too intrusive, when I heard my phone vibrating:

"I didn't think you would remember me! Unfortunately, I had to leave for work the next day, now I'm in Sydney for a couple of months. I would like to take a crash course if that's okay with you. I am free every night at six. Let me know! Ryn."

Sydney. I had always wanted to visit Australia, but I never had a good reason to do so. That seemed crazy enough. Leaving for another continent for a stranger I met and spoke to for two minutes outside a jazz bar. Why not! In the end, traveling was number one on my list!

I started looking for visa requirements on the internet and submitted the form online.

'The processing time is up to 36-48 hours.'

That sucks. However, a few minutes later, I received an email: VISA ACCEPTED and off I could go! I could immediately appreciate Australian efficiency!

Without thinking twice, I bought the cheapest ticket. It was "just" seven hours by plane from Bali and it was low season. I packed my suitcase feeling dreamy and somewhat melancholic, with the intense orange-red background of my last Balinese sunset and, before going to bed, I wrote the last message to Ryn:

"Except for tomorrow night, six o'clock is fine. However, if you like, I should arrive in Sydney in time for a drink, around eight. See you in front of the Opera House?"

Well, now I'm stuck, I thought. Actually, I could have sent it to her before I bought the ticket, but whatever, in the worst case I would have seen a new place.

"Wow, you're here too? Anyway, at eight I can't..."

There you go. Nice job asshole.

"Let’s make nine o'clock. See you tomorrow!"

20.

The flight to Sydney was at a time that should have been illegal: six in the morning precisely.

I think I slept an hour throughout the night, between my state of excitement and the awareness of the madness of my gesture that was beginning to become a reality. But once I had gone through all the various stages and sat on the plane (and especially after my double espresso), my good mood returned.

And here we are, where we started from. Seven hours and two Avengers movies later, I had landed in Australia. The sun was beautiful and the sky was clear, like the Italian one on a late spring day. I wonder how Alberto and Elisa were doing over there.

After a moment of nostalgia, I took the metro to the city centre. It was the green line, it was very clean and tidy, with double-decker carriages and reclining seats, depending on the direction of the train. I always thought that public transport could tell you a lot about a place and Sydney made a good impression on me right away.

I got off at the stop in Ashfield, where I had booked a room in an apartment on Airbnb, one of the cheapest in the area, for the price of two nights in a villa in Bali; the cost of living here was much more expensive. I found myself in a sort of Chinatown, where English was the secondary language.

The landlady had left me instructions on how to get the keys and check-in. Once I entered the apartment, I was shocked. I had never been too squeamish and lived in tiny, cramped up little storage rooms in the worst suburbs of London, but this beat it all: there was stuff scattered everywhere, pots in the sink that had been dirty for weeks, a broken piano in the middle of the hallway with a series of unidentified dusty objects piled up, cockroaches high-fiving each other and a fresh turd sticking out of the toilet.

I tried to contact the landlady several times, but she did not answer. It was already half-past seven in the evening and I had no time to look for an alternative, I had to get ready to meet Ryn. I decided that I would close my eyes for one night and the next day I would look for an alternative, at the moment there were more important things to think about.

I took a shower with my flip flops on and put on my best shirt. I bathed myself in perfume, in case that smelly room had soaked my clothes with its deadly scent and finally I got out of that pigsty.

I came out of the subway right in front of the pier and it was even more impressive than I had imagined. The Opera House overlooked the surrounding sea and the streetlamps illuminated the street before it, with seagulls, curious tourists and street artists playing with fire, literally.

I was punctual; at nine o'clock I was in front of the main entrance. I told her to meet me there because it was also the only place I knew in Sydney.

After twenty minutes, she still hadn't shown up. I sat on a bench lighting a cigarette, while I thought about the absurdity of the situation I had entered. And I started smiling. How many would have done it? I had followed my guts feelings instead of my brain and I was in one of the most beautiful and coveted cities in the world, chasing a stranger, who perhaps would not even show up. It was a wonderful feeling!

Another twenty minutes went by and there was no trace of Ryn. I didn't even have her number, which I hadn't asked her for fear of being intrusive. Probably, not a smart choice, but certainly discreet. After the third cigarette, I stood up and accepted that she was not coming.

I knew I shouldn't have expected anything, but after all, I was hoping for it; I was filled with sadness as I stared at the last ferry back to the pier.

I had never trusted anyone, who knows what had convinced me to do it that time.

One last look at the Opera House for safety and I walked towards the metro. It had been a nice journey in my mind, however, which had led me to discover Australia. While immersed in my thoughts, I was about to climb the steps of the metro in dismay, I thought I heard a familiar voice.

"OLIVER!!"

I turned around...RYN! It was really her, with a tight black dress covering her hips, glamorous red lips and a pair of shiny silver open toed heels, more beautiful than ever before. I was visibly surprised and didn't know what to say. My gloomy mood had suddenly changed.

"Forgive me, I had a business dinner that went on for longer than expected and didn't know how to warn you".

"No problem. You made the scene even more dramatic and perfect!"

"Haha! I didn't expect to see you again! What are you doing in Sydney?"

"I was wondering the same thing myself until a few minutes ago! Anyway, let's go, I'll tell you all about it later."

We entered the bar of the Opera House. The light was soft and there was an engaging atmosphere, with the tables lit by candles and a spectacular view of the ocean.

I told her a bit about myself, my past and recent adventures.

She listened in attentive silence, without saying a word. Her eyes had an exotic, perfect shape and her gaze was intense and warm. I had not yet managed to figure her out and I was dying to know about her.

"Now that I have told you the story of my life, tell me who you are. I'm not particularly interested in your work, but in knowing who Ryn is".

"Well, I'll tell you. My life is probably much more boring than yours. I grew up in the city of Busan, the second largest in South Korea after Seoul. I studied to the point of being sick, just to make my father happy and start working for a company that I have no interest in, but that at least allows me to travel often and see many different places. I am passionate about art and photography, although I almost never have time to dedicate myself to it as I would like. I really envy you for the life you lead and I've always dreamt of it, but I've never had the courage to throw it all away".

"At first it's not easy. You need to get to the point where you realise that, after all, the only thing you have to lose is the rest of your unhappy life. Once I did that, dropping everything and starting over was more natural."

"I wish I had your light heartedness and determination. Anyway, you still haven't told me what you're doing in Sydney".

"I care about the success of my students, so I follow them closely!"

"Haha! A very thoughtful teacher!"

I got away with that joke and she didn't ask any more questions about it. I couldn't tell her that I was only there to meet her, she would have taken me for a crazy stalker.

"How long are you staying here?"

"I don't know exactly yet. We just started a new brand and service project in Australia, that's what I do. I promote the company and its development in various countries. I think it's going to take me two or three months to launch it here, because of the hustle and bustle."

"Fantastic. And why do you want to learn Italian?"

"My company's main office in Europe is in Italy, so I am often there, and I am tired of looking like an idiot with a translator next to me every time there is a meeting. We generally speak in English, but the director is an old lady, incredibly talented in her job, though who can't speak English very well and there are often communication issues".

"I understand. Don't worry, I take it as a personal commitment, at the next business meeting you will sound like a native!"

“Haha! I'm counting on it!"

We continued to talk about this and that until the waiters threw us out. I walked her to the cab stand.

"It seems to me that I have already lived this scene".

"It is true. Too bad you are on foot; I might have accepted a ride this time. Now you are officially a stranger who I trust a little bit!"

"I am honoured! It was good to see you again, Ryn. So… I’ll speak to you tomorrow for the first lesson!"

"Certainly! I had a great time too. Good night Oliver!"

Normally I would have asked her to come and finish the

evening with me, but with her, I didn't have the courage. And I didn't even have a decent place to take her.

It was 2am and I was falling asleep. In half an hour by bus, I was able to return to Ashfield. On the way back to my room, that lair of horrors, I could see a couple of local animals. Crossing a tree-lined avenue, I felt something like a quick flutter of wings. I looked up but saw nothing. A few seconds later, I had the same feeling. Still nothing.

"Watch out for the BATMANS, man! If they catch you, you have to jump into the ocean!", exclaimed a drunken homeless man sitting on the sidewalk. I didn't even have time to look up and saw one of these giant bats drop a bomb. In the blink of an eye, I found myself with shit on all over my pants and my shoes.

I later discovered that they were *flying foxes*; they looked like giant bats and measured about one and a half a foot.

"Hahaha!! I told you, man!! They are fucking snipers!"

Fantastic. I hurried back to my apartment before the shit dried. The lights weren't working properly either, it looked like the set of a film by Alfred Hitchcock.

I was so tired that I didn't even have the strength to think about where I was, I just wanted to sleep; it was very hot, so I took off my clothes, rinsed them in the wash basin and went to bed. When I was about to close my eyes, I started hearing noises from the room next door. Voices of a man and a woman speaking Chinese.

I realised that, in reality, that apartment originally had only one bedroom, to which a plywood partition had been added in the middle, probably glued with double-sided tape, to divide the room and create another one. I knocked on the fake wall and they stopped talking for about ten minutes. I was about to fall asleep again and I began to hear moans louder and louder.

'Well, let's give them this moment of glory, they'll finish, sooner or later.' And instead, the guy was really into it, the woman kept screaming louder and louder until she even started banging on the wall. Confused, I turned on the light to understand what was going on, just in time to see the plywood wall coming down on the floor, also crushing a two-inch cockroach that was happily crawling around the room, oblivious to its imminent end.

The scene in front of me was worthy of a gang-bang: me naked on the bed, a bent over whale and his little cock staring at me, speechless. The three of us looked at each other for a few seconds without opening our mouths, until he came out with a very sober "Sorry!", and, as if it was nothing, took the plywood wall in his hand, put it back in place...And kept going on for another half hour!

Rampant cockroaches, shitting mega-bats and horny Chinese; that's how my trip to Australia began.

21.

The next day, as soon as I woke up, I escaped from that dump. I still had the employee discount from my previous chain of luxury hotels where I had worked in London; somehow, they forgot to remove me from the system. Normally, I wouldn't have taken advantage of it, but it was a matter of necessity, given the crazy prices in Sydney. And then, after a night in there, I deserved it.

I managed to book a week in one of the most luxurious hotels in the city, paying only thirty dollars per night, including breakfast. I immediately went to check-in. It was located in one of the most central areas of the city, a few blocks from the *Town Hall* stop, in the main street, where you'd find every kind of store and restaurant chain.

When I arrived at the reception, I stood in line, while a lady was complaining, shouting and dramatically insulting the guy on duty, because of a satellite channel that could not be seen well. I laughed. Oh, how I did not miss these absurdities and daily frustrations. Who knows what a meaningless life that woman must have had to create such a little theatrical performance for such a stupid reason.

They gave me a room on the twelfth floor with a view of the city, with a huge bed and television, a cocktail table and bathtub. Definitely better than my previous room. I immediately took a bath to disinfect myself from any possible bacterial infection I could have got from my previous stay and did some work for a few hours, giving a couple of video lessons, publishing an article on my website and then I went out to explore the city.

Many of the neighbourhoods had names identical to those of London: Waterloo, Kensington, Paddington, King's Cross... Sydney undoubtedly had a decidedly Anglo-Saxon touch in its socio-cultural and architectural structure, which told of its clear British origins, despite a much more pleasant climate.

I decided to start from Coogee beach. It was strange for me to go from the skyscrapers in the centre to a white sandy beach overlooking the ocean and I was pleasantly impressed. Walking along the promenade, I came to a path surrounded by trees and exotic plants, that led to a protected natural park open to everyone: a two miles' walk on the cliffs, surrounded by greenery, overlooking the Tasman Sea and offering a unique and harmonious panorama.

That view managed to stop my thoughts for an instant. I still did not have a well-defined plan in mind, but that moment alone, was worth the price of the ticket.

I spent half an hour observing the pristine landscape and I walked another three miles, until I found myself at famous Bondi Beach. It was very similar to Coogee, only much bigger and messier, surrounded by a huge green space and with many more people and chaos.

Soon, I decided to go elsewhere. I was very curious to see a koala up close, so I took the bus to the nearest wildlife reserve, which was an hour and twenty minutes away. The name of it was, in fact, Koala Park, a bit pretentious thinking about it now, there were hundreds of strange animals that I didn't even know existed and only two koalas in the whole park; but it was worth it anyway. The happiness you get from holding a "cuddly teddy bear" in your arms is indescribable, it generates uncontrollable tenderness and joy.

I was also lucky enough to be able to play with kangaroos; certainly, interesting animals, despite the fact that every now and then they start to punch with their paws for no good reason.

I lost track of time and when I looked at the clock it was already five o'clock. I hurried back to the hotel; I had my first video lesson with Ryn at six. I combed my hair and dressed almost to perfection, with my jacket and a white shirt unbuttoned. I felt a bit ridiculous, but after all, why not. I turned on the computer and, right on time, Ryn called me. She was just as beautiful as usual, with her hair untied, perfectly straight and shiny, that hid her candid and smiling face.

"Good evening! Are you going to a party?"

"No, I'm a top teacher. The presentation is important!"

"Haha! What an impeccable service! Very well, let us begin, Professor Oliver!"

We began to talk about this and that naturally. I discovered that she was the same age as me, that she loved pizza and sunsets. Her level of Italian was already excellent and she had an Asian accent that made her even more adorable. When she read a particularly difficult sentence, I smiled and she noticed it.

"Laughing at me professor?”

"Haha no, you're very cute when you speak Italian."

"This service is less professional than I expected, you know?!" she said, blushing and smiling at the same time.

"Maybe I could make it up to you with a pizza and a view of the sunset..."

"This is even less professional, professor"

"Absolutely not, it's a reward for your dedication."

"Haha! You really are a top teacher!"

At that moment her phone rang. Looking at the screen, she

babbled something like *abeoji.*

"Excuse me, Oliver, I have to take this call. We'll be in touch."

And she ended the video call. Goddamn Abeoji, whoever it was. I wish I knew who the hell called her. Maybe a friend. Or worse, the boyfriend. The idea that there was somebody in her life had never crossed my mind before, but the opposite seemed absurd at the time. How could such a beautiful, intelligent and bright girl not be taken? Maybe I did not want to think about it before because I would have hated the idea that she was with someone else. She had entered in a few moments into my innermost dreams, which were crumbling just as quickly.

I tried not to think about it, after all, they were nothing but negative assumptions of my imagination and I went out for dinner. The door of the room in front of mine opened at the same time and... There was Ryn. We looked at each other, surprised for a few moments and burst out laughing.

"I swear I am not a stalker!"

"Haha! The evidence suggests otherwise! What are you

doing here?"

"I'm staying here, I arrived this morning. Where are you going?"

"I got hungry after our intense lesson"

"If you wish, my invitation is still valid, Miss Ryn."

"Uhm...All right professor, but today I choose the place myself!"

She took me to an Italian pizzeria at Darling Harbour, which vaguely reminded me of the Marina Bay district in Singapore; there were several hotels, pubs, restaurants, the Ferris wheel, a few boats and a view of the city's skyscrapers, divided by a water basin in the middle. The sunset and artificial lights of the various skyscrapers created a perfect atmosphere.

We ordered our pizzas and a couple of beers. I tried not to dwell on her choice of Hawaiian pizza with slices of pineapple and ham. After finishing the first pint, I found the courage to ask her who this *abeoji* was.

"Haha are you jealous?"

"Could be"

"Haha! He is the only man in my life"

Fuck. I knew it. What an idiot, all this mess and she's already taken.

" *Abeoji*...It means father in my language."

"Ah...! And what do I know? I just worry about my students!"

I was visibly relieved and she realised it, pretending not to notice.

"Do you reserve this treatment for all of your students?"

"Absolutely not, only the most deserving. On the contrary, I started the loyalty program with prizes very recently, you are the first!"

“Haha, I want to believe it!"

We finished our dinner and she took me up to the deck that overlooks the marina. It was nine o'clock on an ordinary Saturday night, but there were a lot of people gathered there waiting, however I still didn't know what for.

"I remember that you like coloured lights and shiny things in general, so I have a surprise for you!"

After a few seconds, a sudden noise in the sky made me jump and a series of fireworks started to light up the sky above Darling Harbour. I was really amazed and impressed, also by the fact that she remembered that ephemeral detail revealed without any pretence.

"Beautiful, isn't it? "

"Wonderful! But what are they celebrating?"

"Nothing, they do them every Saturday evening at nine o'clock. But it's the first time I've seen them, the other times I came to Sydney I had no one to go with. I am glad you are here."

I looked into her eyes and smiled. My heart was racing. I took her face in my hands and kissed her. At that moment everything was magically perfect, like the scene in a movie.

After the fireworks, we walked to the hotel. We arrived in front of our rooms and looked a little embarrassed.

"My house or your house?!", I sarcastically but hopefully

asked.

“Haha! Don't even think about it! Anyway, thank you for dinner and your pleasant company Professor Oliver, I had a very good time tonight. Good night."

She kissed me again and went into her room.

It was really happening. I was over the moon. I stood on the bed, watching the skyscrapers lit up from my window. I couldn't think of anything else but what had just happened, constantly reliving those scenes in my mind and smiling like a dummy.

After a good half hour of self-contemplation, my cell phone vibrated. I opened the message.

“Are you asleep?”

“No...”

“I can't either. Will you come and keep me company?”

I knocked on her door and found myself in the presidential suite, with three bedrooms, two bathrooms, a living room, a Jacuzzi with televisions everywhere, even in the shower.

"Wow...Your company treats you well!"

"I know the hotel manager and I'm a regular customer, so he upgraded me. But it's too big for me, it's wasted. You can stay here if you want, choose a room".

"Can I stay in that one?"

"That's mine"

"Exactly"

"Haha! All right, you can stay here with me tonight."

We laid on the bed in each other's arms, looking at the city from the highest point, with some jazz playing in the background, until we fell asleep. I haven't slept so well in a long time. Or maybe I had never slept as well as that night.

We woke up early, still as cuddled up as when we had fallen asleep and went to a café across the ocean for breakfast. Ryn looked radiant and her almond-shaped eyes were glowing, spreading joy all around.

We walked along the shore for about fifteen minutes, holding hands, warmed by the first rays of the sun.

Then we took the ferry to *Manly*, a quiet suburb in the north of Sydney, where even the beaches were much more secluded and less crowded. We walked for about twenty minutes on a path surrounded by plants, finding ourselves on an almost deserted beach that came straight out of the bush and we decided to stop there.

"So, tell me, how is your life in Busan?"

"Frantic and stressful. Sometimes I have to work on Sundays too. I haven't seen my high school friends for ages. The only people I hang out with are my colleagues. You know, in Korea, even after the day is over, you go very often to dinner or drinks with the whole team to keep talking about how the various projects are going".

"Terrible...! How can you stand such a situation?"

She looked down, and she lowered her eyes to the sand.

"In Korea that's normal. We've been studying like crazy since childhood, in order to be able to excel and, one day, secure a job in a big company, which guarantees the maximum social prestige. From the moment you enter one of them, your life almost no longer exists, it belongs to them until you retire. If you are lucky, you can rest at the weekend from time to time and during the holidays, but it is not guaranteed. You have, by law, two weeks of vacation a year, but it is almost impossible to get even one in a row. The work that you do in Korea represents your whole life".

"It is pure madness. I guess it's not easy for you to realise this and continue on in spite of everything."

"It is not. But I try to enjoy every moment outside of the usual routine. I, however, compared to many people, am privileged!"

"In what sense?"

"Let's go for a swim, come on!"

She got up in a flash and ran towards the shore. Who knows what she had wanted to say.

We jumped into the water and went back to laugh at whatever rubbish we could think of. I stopped for a second to admire the beauty of her smiling and carefree face. These were wonderful days, that I would never have lived if I hadn't had the courage to leave my few certainties behind me and dive into the absolute void.

Around five o'clock, we got dressed and went back to the hotel for a coffee. After an hour, she was hungry again. She was so slim but ate all the time, I couldn't figure out how it was possible.

"Is it okay if we eat in the room tonight? I am tired and I have to get up early in the morning".

"Of course, your room is as big as a restaurant in Bali!"

"Haha perfect!"

She had found a restaurant in the city that prepared extra-large pizzas and we had two delivered; they were so big that I couldn't even finish mine, but of course, she took care of it.

I sat on the couch to digest and she took another box out of the fridge.

"Are you still hungry?!"

"No, this is a surprise for you!"

Inside the package was a cake with my name on it.

"Happy birthday dear Oliver!"

Hell, it was my birthday and I completely forgot about it.

"But...How did you know...?!"

"It's written on your profile, right under your picture. It struck me that it was in these days!"

I was astonished, confused and moved. I would never have expected this.

"I don't know what to say... You are simply fantastic! Thank you from the bottom of my heart! You are the most beautiful birthday gift that I could wish for."

She smiled at me and I hugged her tightly.

"Your gifts are not over yet!"

She took off her robe and dragged me onto the bed, taking off my clothes and starting to kiss me all over my body. Her skin was soft and velvety, and smelled of powdered sugar.

She climbed on top of me, slipped off her panties and we started making love. Again and again, until, exhausted, we fell asleep holding each other.

My thirty-second year began brilliantly. It was the year of my turning point, which would be much bigger than I had imagined.

22.

The next morning, I woke up late, with a note next to my pillow:

"Good morning Oliver! You were sleeping so well that I didn't want to wake you up. I'm off to work, see you for dinner. Kisses, Ryn."

I spent the day enjoying the comforts of the suite. Every now and then it was just nice to enjoy it. Ryn came home around seven, down in the face.

"Hey…What is it?"

"Tomorrow morning I have to be in Korea, I was called back for an urgent job. My flight leaves in four hours."

I felt those words like a punch in the stomach. I didn't really know what to say. Until a few minutes earlier I was on the moon and suddenly I found myself underground.

"But...We have just met...You can't leave already. I only came here to meet you again..."

"Do you really mean it...?"

"Never been more serious. I was aware of the madness of my gesture, but I chose to come anyway. Don't ask me why, but I felt something inside, I wanted to give us a chance".

"It's the most romantic thing anyone has ever done for me. Unfortunately, however, I cannot say no. And there's something else I have to talk to you about."

She stopped for a moment, looking away and lowering her eyes.

"So?"

"Everything between us was so magical and spontaneous that I forgot for a moment the reality from which I came. I am the daughter of the president of Kaiwon. It is a multinational company that produces software and specialised programmes and has a lot of political relevance in my country. My father has an agreement with the president of another large company for an upcoming merger. And his son is my fiancé, even though we hardly ever see each other. Do you understand that I can't afford to screw this up?"

Kaiwon. That name wasn't new to me, but at that moment I couldn't remember where I had heard it.

I was visibly shocked and disappointed by her words. I didn't want to believe it. Everything had happened so quickly and that moment of happiness was already dissolving as quickly as it had come.

"So, let me get this straight...I was just a distraction, a hobby or something else?"

"I don't know...You weren't meant to be. You suddenly entered my life, which is totally planned from now until the next twenty years, without even giving me time to realise it. You made me feel as if you really cared about me and it was as if you could read me deeply. You didn't even care what I was doing, which is what most people come to me for; all you cared about was being with me. No one had ever treated me this way and made me feel special, because of who Ryn is and not because I am the daughter of President

Sung".

"I find it hard to accept all this. And emotionally I don't want to believe it. However, from a purely logical point of view, I understand the situation. And I will avoid making a pathetic scene where I beg you to stay or try to convince you to do so, because I know that, even with good reasons, you wouldn't do it".

"That's exactly what I'm talking about. That's why it's so difficult to let you go. I have been happy in these last few days together, as never before in my life. Thank you for everything, Oliver."

She hastily packed her suitcase and, turning to me with one last look full of sadness and sorrow that filled her little almond-shaped eyes that I liked so much, she closed the door behind her.

I sat there in silence, sitting on the sofa in the presidential suite, staring into space, trying to understand how and why, or more simply, trying to accept reality, that wonderful dream that suddenly became a bad nightmare from which I could not wake up.

It is always hard to let go of that which, even for a short time, had made you happy, especially if you had never been happy before. No, this time I wouldn't be able to just forget it with a couple of beers and a re-bound; I would be hung up on her for a while.

I poured myself a glass of whiskey, watched the sunset and toasted to her, to the emotions she had given me in such a short time, which I will cherish forever in my heart; to her, who for a second had caressed my soul and taught me what it meant to love a woman.

I didn't even care that she had someone else, in fact, I was grateful to her for everything she had allowed me to live.

I spent four hours on that couch. I didn't even have dinner and the bottle of whiskey was empty. I took one last look at Sydney's brightly lit sky and saw a plane in the distance taking off. I wondered if it was hers. I drank the last sip and started to cry. I went into our bedroom and smelled her pillow, savouring the scent of powdered sugar one last time.

I felt really pathetic and helpless. I stole another bottle from the minibar, after all, at least she owed me that, and went back to my double room. I hadn't decided what I would do next, but I didn't want to stay in that suite anymore.

I was so drunk that I fell asleep as soon as my face touched the pillow. And I slept on it for thirteen hours.

When I woke up, it was not like the other times, it still hurt. However, I have always been a practical person, and I forced myself to believe that, somehow, I would have to start over. I had two more days booked and paid for in Sydney and then I would think about it.

At that moment, I certainly needed a friendly voice, so I called Alberto for words of comfort. I told him all my misadventures in the recent months, including the latest madness for Ryn.

"Damn Oliver! I am sorry for Ryn. But despite everything, you are living an incredible life! I am still here, every single day, slicing ham and mincing meat…!"

A voice in the background interrupted him:

"Alberto! Who the fuck is calling you at 5 am?"

"Dad, come on, it's Oliver, he's calling me from

Australia..."

"A man, not even a chick. You are going in the wrong direction lately, I am telling you!"

I burst out laughing.

"Excuse me Oliver, let me go make some coffee, or else I'll be dealing with drama over here. Anyway, I was thinking, why don't you try writing a book about all these fantastic adventures? If you are still able to write! I think it would be successful. I'll even write the preface for free!"

"Haha! I will think about it! See you soon buddy, hang in there!"

"Always!"

That call had calmed me down a bit, as usual when I was talking to him. I thought about his words without initially giving it much consideration. The idea did appeal to me, but I was not in the mood, nor did I know where to begin.

I decided to go back to Asia first. The cost of living in Sydney was really high and I had no reason to stay there anymore. But I didn't even want to go back to Bali, for me it was over this time. There was a country that had always fascinated me and it seemed the right time to go there: Thailand. Yes, I liked the idea right away. I organised my things and the next morning I was sitting on a plane to Phuket.

23.

After a nine hours' flight, I finally landed in Thailand. As soon as I got off the plane, I inhaled deeply; it was the tropical air of South-East Asia, that unmistakable warm-humid wind that gives you a sense of well-being as soon as you arrive.

Mindful of the Balinese experience, I had booked a local cab before arriving, to avoid the crowds of unlicensed taxi drivers on the way out again.

Phuket is a huge island, full of wonderful places and hidden gems, which can change from one neighbourhood to another; it is also a renowned destination for stereotypical tourists, famous for its transgressions to the limit of legality, or often even beyond.

I chose the area of Karon Beach, upon the advice of a

former colleague of mine. There was a good mix of services offered, nightlife and quiet and uncrowded areas, with a beautiful beach that stretched for several miles.

My hotel stood on a slight plateau and my room was completely covered with wood, including the base of the bed; it had a desk, a minifridge and a cosy balcony with a small table, overlooking the sea. It was perfect to serve my needs and cost just the equivalent of eleven pounds per night.

It was already late in the evening and I had not eaten yet. I went into the main street looking for food and found a cart with an old lady roasting fish on the grill. There were no tables, but with just two euros I took home all the fish, seasoned with lime and a local hot sauce; it was the most delicious I had ever tasted in my life!

I saw only extremely happy and worry-free people around. It was as if they had kept intact that innate joy for life and its little things, which Westerners take for granted.

They had a naturally higher tone of voice than in Bali, perhaps also because of the language and they also seemed more like "hot blooded" people. I could see them getting upset over basically nothing and, two seconds later, laughing happily again.

They were also much more shameless, they would throw themselves into the street, trying to invite you into their stores or bars without any kind of problem, showing off their big smiles with thirty-two teeth and accompanying you inside arm in arm.

And that's how they caught me too. After dinner, I felt alone in that empty room, still thinking about Ryn, so I decided to go out and explore the local bars.

At the end of the main street, there was a side street where all the bars in the neighbourhood were located. Most of them were very simple, in a semi-open space, with a counter, stools, a pool table, tons of beer and lots of half-naked girls playing and inviting you to sit with them. At another time I would have been enthusiastic about it, but there at that moment, I didn't feel like it.

In the end, I chose a bar at the end of the street, where they played live music in a seemingly more sober environment.

A beautiful girl at the entrance accompanied me to the table, putting her arm around my waist and handing me the menu. I managed to free myself from her tentacles, making her understand that it was not a good time, and she left.

The whole staff was looking at me; it was made up only of young, provocative and barely dressed girls. I was also the youngest customer in there, among all the over-fifties looking for fun. I, on the other hand, that night, just wanted to drink and listen to music to numb my thoughts.

I ordered a five-litre tower of Chang, the iconic local beer, and sat on the sofa to enjoy the "concert". The singers were pretty good and had a lot of interesting songs in their repertoire, some of my all-time favourites, like *Oasis' Don't Look Back In Anger*, *Mr Brightside* from *The Killers* and *Mardy Bum* from the *Arctic Monkeys*, which I enjoyed to the max, one glass after another.

Chang's characteristic was to be perceived as a very light beer and, without realising it, in one hour I had already drunk five litres of beer. I still felt sober and decided to have a second one. I continued to drink, this time more slowly and, after the seventh litre, I became even more sociable. I started talking to a girl who barely understood me, but still seemed to enjoy our time. I found out shortly afterwards that she was not a girl, but he/she was still good company.

Meanwhile, the place was emptying out, with the other "waitresses" who had convinced their fatties to take them to the hotel and continue their evening there. I saw the last couple going out; he must have been sixty, she was a little over twenty.

In Thailand, I had a different perception of paid sex. Although it was certainly not a well-considered practice, nor legal, they were far less judgmental about it, it was as if it was part of their everyday life. And, at least for what I could see that evening, it was by choice, without suffering passively; it was like a form of exchange: a sort of "donation" in exchange for a nice evening and you both come out happy and smiling.

Many girls gave me that impression, apart from one of them, who was sitting there at the counter with her resigned gaze, the last girl left. She was very pretty, olive skin, long black hair and fleshy lips; her name was Khwan and she was about thirty years old. She asked me if I wanted to go out with her.

"Forget it doll! I've never paid a woman in my life and I'm not starting today. But if you want, you can sit with me and keep me company".

"Okay. Buy me a drink?"

"So be it. Have a glass, we still have three litres here!"

I wish I never said that. She drained two and a half litres of beer in just under half an hour and we ordered five more. She told me she came from Bangkok, where she was selling chicken skewers with a cart in the city centre and had moved to the island in the hope of meeting a "*falang*", a foreigner who would take her away with him and guarantee her a happy and financially stable life. She said that it was a common dream of many girls in Thailand, especially in touristy places, who saw every foreign tourist as their potential Richard Gere from *Pretty Woman*, who would take them out of economic precariousness and give them a luxurious life in a better place, not imagining that most of us were just as poor, but merely lucky that our currency had a very favourable exchange rate there.

Between one litre of beer and another, it was four o'clock in the morning and we were blind drunk. I walked to the hotel and Khwan followed me.

"Look, I don't have much money and I'm in love with another girl, so you're just wasting your time with me."

"Can I come anyway? I don't feel like going home..."

Inebriated by alcohol, I accepted. I didn't even feel like arguing, I just wanted to sleep.

We went into my room and she undressed me completely. It would have been noble of me to refuse, but I did not. She unbuttoned her dress, remaining completely naked and came on top of me. She screamed so loud that I was ashamed of it, for fear of being heard from the neighbouring rooms. I remained still, half alive half dead on the bed.

After a couple of minutes, I moved her aside and got up.

"I apologise. I can't do it, I'm still thinking about another person".

She looked at me surprised and a little embarrassed, getting dressed quickly.

"I've never had a guy ask me to stop before".

"I hadn't had that happen to me either."

"Don't you like me?"

"You are very beautiful and I feel like an idiot. I just can't do it."

"Your girlfriend is very lucky to have you."

"Yeah, she just doesn't know it."

We went to the balcony to smoke a cigarette, while the dawn was breaking on the horizon.

"Why are you doing this?"

"Why do I do what?"

"Sex for money. I don't want to say the prostitute, because you are not, and it shows."

"It's a difficult situation...", she said, embarrassed, looking away.

But when I drink, I become even more insolent than usual,

and I also lose those few remaining filters between my brain and my mouth.

"Do you, by any chance, have children?"

She just looked away and burst into tears, hiding her face in her hands. I felt a lot of compassion for her and like an insensitive idiot at the same time. After all, who gave me the right to judge her, I knew nothing about her or her daily battles.

"I'm sorry, I'm a very nosy man. Here, have some water."

"Thank you. Anyway yes, I have a little girl, she stayed in Bangkok with my mother and I send her money to study every week. Her father ran away with another woman and left us alone; he also took the food cart and all our savings, so I found myself doing this".

"I'm sorry, it's a very sad story. But you didn't find anything else?"

"Unfortunately, no. I can't do anything except cook, but no restaurants would hire me. I couldn't even go to school, because my mother needed me for the food cart and I started working there when I was very young. But my daughter gives me the strength to go on every day. I am saving up to buy another cart, then I can go back to her. Slowly we will rise up again."

"How much does a trolley cost?"

"Five thousand dollars"

"And how much more do you need to buy it?"

"A little more than a thousand why?"

I thought about it a few seconds. It was a big figure and, as usual, I didn't have much to spare. But every time I got into trouble, I was always helped by some stranger; it was my turn to become someone else's hero.

"Here it is. It was my budget for two months, but it means I'll be drinking a little less in the next few days!"

She opened her eyes wide, still incredulous, mouth wide open; then she hugged me strongly, bursting into tears again and thanking me repeatedly. Her reaction filled my heart, I really hoped that she would make it.

Meanwhile, the sun was already high in the sky and we

decided to go for breakfast.

"Come, I'll take you to a good place. It's on me!"

She took me to a hidden alley five minutes from my hotel, where there was a food truck that served only pad-thai, a very simple and tasty local dish, made of noodles with seafood and crushed peanuts. It was delicious and cost the equivalent of eighty pence! It was one of the strangest breakfasts ever, but I will never forget it. And probably not even Khwan.

"I have to go. Thanks for everything Oliver, you have changed my life. I hope one day to meet a guy like you. When I will reopen my food cart, you are always welcome to come and eat for free!"

“Haha! I am counting on it! Take care of yourself Khwan, best of luck!"

She kissed me on the lips and left.

That same evening, after dinner, I passed by the same bar where I had met her and took a peek inside. There were the usual fat wolves in tank tops and half-naked waitresses, but not Khwan. I smiled and went back to my room. It was time to get to work.

I kept thinking about Ryn, but with a little more ease. Who knows where she was, how she was and if she still remembered me. I took a long sigh and started to slap myself; I made up my mind that I should just concentrate on myself and work hard. Oh yes, I was going to show her, she would have heard about me in Korea too.

I turned on the pc, accompanied by a still vivid hangover and I started to throw down everything I had inside.

I was locked in that room for two months, spending the entire rainy season indoors and going out just to eat and buy beers.

One morning, I woke up and found a message from Khwan on my cell phone: a picture behind her new cart, with her mother and daughter next to it and a small sign that read "Oliver's chicken skewers", radiant with happiness:

“Hi Oliver, we are open! When you pass by Bangkok, remember to come and visit us! A big hug, Khwan”.

This is the memory I have of Thailand, an apparently relaxed reality, where anything can happen in one night, constant comings and goings between heaven and hell, where all is more intense, like the colours of the sunset, the emotions and the life itself. Always, with a huge, big smile.

24.

Sometime later, I moved to Malaysia, on the island of Langkawi, passing through Kuala Lumpur, where I stayed for just one night: one of the craziest places I had ever visited, with endless traffic and huge skyscrapers, stretching all over the city and whose end could not be seen.

In Langkawi it was a different story. It was still not very popular and absolutely peaceful. The whole island could be visited driving around by scooter in little more than four hours, finding deserted streets with palm trees and shrubs along the sea, for a completely regenerating experience.

I also allowed myself a visit to the beach of Tanjung Rhu, also semi-deserted, and took the cable car to the Sky Bridge, one hundred and twenty-five metres long located on top of a green mountain, from which you could enjoy a heavenly view. I also tried to go to the biggest club on the island, during one of the breaks from me being antisocial, but I found only eight people there, with whom I was able to exchange only a few words anyway.

Also, Langkawi has, for reasons still unknown to me, very low tax on alcohol, so it turned out to be incredibly cheap. It was, in short, the perfect place to work undisturbed.

In just over three months, I finished writing my book. I spent as many months as possible reviewing it and finding ways to publish it. I had put a lot of hope into it and was convinced that I had done an acceptable job, but I didn't know what to expect.

Finally, after waiting for what seemed like forever, the release date was set: the twenty-third of November.

It was an unexpected success. In less than a month, I had already sold over a thousand copies and people began to get curious about the author as well, which gave more and more visibility to my online newspaper. That unexpected dream, hidden and underestimated, was materialising and I was over the moon.

A few days later, I received a call from my editor:

"Good morning Oliver! We are doing great! With Christmas coming up, it's time to push it even further".

"What do you mean?"

"I would like you to present your book here, in Rome. Tell me when you would be available, then we'll schedule the event and book your flight and hotel."

At that time, I had just left Langkawi, headed back in Singapore, as I wanted to greet to some old friends and show Marvin my results since our last meeting.

I was excited about that opportunity to go back to Italy after a long time. It was December 16th and I decided to leave immediately. The event was set in one of the bookstores downtown, exactly one week later.

Fifteen endless hours by plane and here I landed at Fiumicino airport, after seven troubled years. At that time, I had left with almost nothing in my pocket, distressed and driven only by a faint hope in my heart, without knowing if or how I would make it; and now I was finally back, somehow, as a winner.

I took a cab to the hotel that had been reserved for me, ironically, once again by the same company I had worked for in London.

On the way, I stopped to observe Rome from the window. It was exactly as I had left it, nothing had changed, except for a few more potholes here and there; but it was still beautiful, even more, decorated and shiny for the Christmas period. And it was a cold that I was no longer used to.

When I arrived at my destination, I unpacked in a few minutes and then I set off for the city. I had a strange feeling after a long time and also a bit of nostalgia.

I went to buy some warm and presentable clothes for the occasion and I took the opportunity to say hello to Alberto, who was still working in his father's butchery nearby. He was even bigger than the last time and wore a white apron with spots of blood everywhere. As soon as he saw me, he dropped what he was doing and came towards me, crushing me with his greasy hands.

"Haha!! Damn you, asshole!! You made it back!"

"I am happy to see you too! How's it going?"

"As usual, I do not have such an exciting life like yours. Also, Elisa always works there at the supermarket as a cashier. We see each other occasionally, but she's always tired and depressed lately and she's got a lot of nervous tics. In short, nothing has changed! You, on the other hand, I have heard that you have made a turn!"

"Yes, the book sales are going very well. The day after tomorrow at six o'clock there is the official presentation at the bookstore across the street, you have to come. And tell that to Elisa as well. I have a surprise for you."

"Really? Knowing you, it will be some bullshit of yours that you use as an excuse to go drinking!"

"No, no, I'm serious. Then we'll go have a drink; it's on me, I owe it to you!"

"Alright then! See you soon, my friend."

I was sleepy, but I didn't want to go to sleep. My desire to "taste the air of home" was not yet satiated. I walked from

Piazza del Popolo to the Trevi Fountain. It always had its charm, especially in the evening, when it was not overcrowded with tourists and completely illuminated. I sat on the steps to savour the moment and tidy up my thoughts.

I was close to one of the most important days of my life, and yet I did not feel so euphoric. I was immensely happy with the direction in which I had managed to take my life and what it was giving me, but something was always missing. Or maybe, someone. I would have liked Dad to be there. And Mum too. An event had been organised just for me, to celebrate my greatest success achieved at that time and I had no one to share it with. And, after a year, I was still thinking about Ryn. I didn't know how or why, but I hadn't felt the same emotions as in that ephemeral time spent with her and I had never forgotten her.

While I was contemplating the fountain, I thought of its famous coin legend: it is said that, by throwing three coins into the water, the first one would guarantee a return to Rome, the second one would bring the love of life and the third one would fulfil one's deepest desire. Without giving it too much consideration, I took three coins from my pockets: ten euro cents, fifty Indonesian rupees and half an Australian dollar. I turned my back and threw them all together, in the unlikely event that the legend was somewhat true.

At the same moment I threw them, I heard another thud in the water. I turned to see who else was as pathetic as me, throwing pennies into a fountain at nine o'clock on an icy December evening and I met at a girl's gaze.

A few seconds of confusion and bewilderment, which left room for a long moment of disbelief: it was Ryn.

'That fountain is very powerful!' I thought to myself.

We looked at each other for a few seconds without being able to say anything, then she slowly came towards me smiling.

"Oliver is it really you?! What are you doing here? It's been a long time!"

"It's a pleasure to see you again, I had hoped for this for so long. I certainly never imagined it would happen here! I arrived this morning. If you accompany me to dinner, I will tell you everything that has happened since you left. I know a place nearby where they prepare unbeatable pizzas!"

She accepted. I told her everything: about my book, my website, Khwan and how much I missed her. She listened to me intently, as she did last time, without saying a word, with her usual serious and attentive look, indicating a half-smile.

"Where did you end up?"

"That day I returned to Korea I was very sad. Meeting you made me think a lot about my life, how I was living it and my future marriage. But there was no revolution like you did, I wasn't able to. I went to the office to my father, who didn't even want to talk about me leaving the company. Three months ago, there was a meltdown in the European market, so he sent me here to monitor the situation. Before I left, I went to my fiancé's house; I wanted to discuss our situation and the fact that I was no longer very sure about our relationship, even though there was a merger of our respective companies. Well, at least that context resolved itself: when I entered his house, I found him in bed with his secretary. I still remember his expression of terror! I should have been furious and started throwing whatever I could find at him, but I didn’t. I felt deeply relieved and left without saying a word. I haven't seen him since and that's okay."

"Wow, that sounds like the plot of a soap opera! So now you live here in Rome?"

"Yes, at least until things are settled. Tomorrow we will have a meeting with the director of Kaiwon Italy and we will see how to proceed. We will also have a refreshment stand open to families from six o'clock onwards, as a corporate Christmas party. Would you like to accompany me?"

"Gladly! But I can't stay long, you know, my book launch is the next day and I don't want to go there too drunk."

"No problem, you can stay as long as you want!"

We finished eating and went out to walk among the decorated windows and the illuminated streets.

"Exactly...What were you doing at the Trevi Fountain at that hour?"

"I was feeling lonely and I went for a walk. As usual, you interfered with my plan!"

"Oh yes? You never seemed to me to be particularly upset for my interference!"

"Haha! Because I am polite!"

"And also, very accommodating, I might add! I would be curious to know two things... The first is: what did you wish for when you threw the coin?"

"I will never tell you!"

“Uhm... Okay, I won't insist. The second, however, you must answer me: why did you never look for me again after all these months?"

"I wanted to be alone for a while. I thought of you often, but I was afraid that you had already met someone else. I didn't want to ruin the beautiful memory I had of us and the moments we spent together".

"Of course, it seemed reasonable; why risk to be happy

when you can bask in your own sadness and loneliness while maintaining a beautiful memory, it makes perfect sense! Well, I'll pretend to believe that!"

"Hahaha! You have not changed your usual cynical and unpleasant attitude!"

"In any case, I am glad to have seen you again. See you tomorrow, then!"

"Sure..."

"'Night!"

"Wait..."

She came towards me and kissed me gently on the lips.

"I am also happy to have met you again. I missed you more than you know. Good night Professor!"

She smiled and left.

'I must visit that blessed fountain more often, I was so close to it then and I underestimated it!' I thought to myself, walking towards my hotel.

For a moment, I felt that everything was slowly settling down. And it wasn't over yet. The next day would be even more memorable.

The next afternoon, I went to visit my publisher to finalise the last details of the event. It took longer than expected and I was late for the Kaiwon Christmas party. At the reception desk, I was greeted by a funny guy with a themed hat and an impassive face.

"Are you part of the Kaiwon team, sir?"

"No, I was invited by Miss Ryn Sung."

His eyes widened and he immediately became more helpful, accompanying me to the entrance of the room, where the party was taking place. When I entered, everyone was applauding, probably a speech on the stage just finished and, immediately afterwards, an orchestra started playing Christmas songs. Finally, I found Ryn, busy entertaining her employees with the usual small talk that nobody cares about.

"Hey you"

"Oliver! I thought you weren't coming anymore!"

"My meeting lasted longer than expected. Did I miss

something?"

"Only the director's speech to the employees, nothing that might interest you."

"It would be interesting to meet her instead, I guess she is a resourceful woman!"

"If you want, I will introduce her to you as soon as I see her around"

"If it happens. Anyway…How are you? How was your day?"

"It’s better, now that you are here. Don't ask me the details, but it was never-ending and I just want to drink and make love to you as soon as this stupid party is over".

"Wow, I wasn't expecting that! Anyway, what makes you think I'd accept after the way you left me last time?"

"The fact that you've been undressing me with your eyes since the moment you arrived..."

It was true. Ryn wore a shiny red dress, low-cut and short, which showed off her legs and emphasised her perfect body. She was the most beautiful of all and I was instantly falling in love with her like a teenager at every look.

"Nothing gets past you"

"You can say that! Come on, let's go celebrate, it's Christmas for us too!"

She took me to the centre of the room, where cocktails were being served. I had everyone's eyes on me, being Miss Sung's plus one; but I must admit that I didn't mind, after all. There must have been at least a hundred people in that room and I felt a bit out of place, but I still tried to enjoy the evening.

Ryn introduced me to some people I had no interest in, but I still tried to look polite. My mind was elsewhere. I kept thinking about where I had heard the name of that company before.

I could hear trivial, incoherent speeches, clouded by their alcohol levels; turnover, new market opportunities, great hypothetical future successes. So much crap. I was sitting there, swallowing one gin-tonic after another, when one of these inane speeches caught my attention.

"Since Ms Ferri took the chair, there has certainly been a turning point in productivity and employees' mood, it's undeniable; that idiot of Floberti got what he deserved!"

Suddenly, my mind cleared up. I reconnected everything. I immediately ran to Ryn, who was chatting with a company executive officer and I took her aside.

"Ryn, what is the name of the director of Kaiwon Italy?"

"Aurora Ferri, why?"

"I need to see her now"

"Oliver, what's wrong with you?"

"I'll explain later, I need to talk to her."

"All right, she'll be around, I'll help you look for her."

I looked for her frantically throughout the room, without success. I went back downstairs to talk to the impassive usher:

"Have you by any chance seen Ms Ferri?"

"Yes, sir, she left just a few seconds ago, perhaps you can still catch up with her".

I rushed out of the building, but she wasn't there. I started running down the street, hoping to meet her. Still nothing. I turned first to the right, then to the left, far and wide.

There was no sign of her. I sat on a bench nearby and started crying, without even knowing why, with my head bent over and my hand over my eyes.

Suddenly I felt a hand caressing my hair. My eyesight was clouded by my tears and it took me a while to focus.

"My Oliver..."

I looked up and there she was, with a few more wrinkles, but always beautiful and with the same sunny and melancholic smile, with eyes full of bitter tears: she was my mother.

I held her tight to me and burst into uncontrollable tears. At that moment I didn't care anymore about anything, about who was right or wrong, about the past pains, the sacrifices and the life I had been forced to live, about the restlessness repressed inside me. I just wanted to stay there, in that embrace that had been taken away from me too soon, enjoying every single moment of it. I let myself be wrapped by her arms, while she sobbed whilst also smiling, with her face lined with tears, holding me tightly to herself, on that cold December night.

I never thought I would meet her again, much less there. There are those who say that, in life, everything happens for a reason, even if until then, I had never believed it all.

After a few minutes, Ryn also arrived, understandably confused.

"Oliver...Do you and Ms Ferri know each other…?"

"I would say yes, even though we haven't seen each other in a while. About twenty-five years."

25.

My mother immediately pulled herself together and we found ourselves in front of each other. It was time for clarification.

"There would be a thousand things to say, tell and specify. But what I want to know most is...Why? Why did you leave, disappear from my life and never look for me again? Do you have any idea what I went through?! How difficult it was to grow up without you? How I felt abandoned and the loneliness I suffered?!"

My words hit the spot. The expression on her face became gloomy and bitter, her eyes swollen with tears. I stared at her undaunted, clouded with anger, waiting for an answer, with Ryn watching, astonished and amazed.

"I apologise Oliver. And I do not deceive myself that it is

enough to forgive my absence and all that you had to go through. I saw what you did and I am very proud of it. You have been so strong...! Just like your father. But you never gave up, you made it. And I never doubted it. Just know that, for what it's worth, I have always carried you in my heart and prayed every night that you would get through it. I had to leave. I did it for you, especially for you."

"You have a great deal of courage to come and tell me these things! How exactly do you think your absence has benefited me?! For having been forced to live like a beggar in a shithole? For having to dine on chocolate bars because I didn't even have enough money for proper food? Or for finding myself an orphan at the age of twenty? Tell me, because I really can't understand!"

My words pierced her like blades through the chest. If on the one hand, I felt sorry to see her like that, on the other hand, she must have known what her abandonment had meant. It had been twenty-five years that I had kept everything inside me and it came out like a flood.

"You have no idea how guilty I felt every single day. I'm not asking you to forgive me, but I just want you to know the truth and fully understand my reasons. Things with your father weren't going well and I was in a nasty business. I decided, for your sake, to leave you out of it. He never forgave me and, even when I tried to contact you, he always told me to stay away, saying that I would only make you suffer. When I learned of his death, I was very sad. As soon as I heard about it, I looked everywhere for you, but no one knew where you were. I am sorry, I am really sorry. We all make mistakes and leaving you was the biggest mistake of my life. I wish I could start over, if you give me the opportunity, even though I know I don't deserve it".

I looked at Ryn, who nodded her head and smiled at me. I squinted my eyelids for a few moments and looked into my mother's weary, tired eyes.

"I don't feel like it. I'm sorry, Mother. Your absence has caused me too much pain. But it was good to see you again and to know that you are well. I wish you the best for your life."

I put on my coat and turned around, walking towards my hotel, while I could hear my mother sobbing. Ryn reached me at a fast pace, tugging at me and telling me to stop.

"Oliver, what are you doing? I don't know the story between the two of you but...She's your mother! Are you leaving her there like that?"

"Come with me, I'll tell you everything. I need to be close to you tonight."

"But..."

"I don't feel like talking about it now, I'll explain later."

"All right. Let me go get my things and I'll join you."

When we got to the hotel, I told her the whole story and she was amazed. She said nothing; she knew it would be useless. She came towards me with a glass of wine in her hand, wrapping me in her warmest embrace.

I was supposed to prepare for the presentation of my book

the next day, but my mind was elsewhere. I could not stop thinking about what had happened. Damn my pride. It had always made me do stupid things. I was right, and overwhelmingly so, in every way. And yet, I realised how little being right matters under certain circumstances.

I was able to sleep for a few hours, just in time to say bye to Ryn, who was going to work.

"Good morning! Ready for the big day?

"No, but I'll make it anyway!"

"I have no doubt!"

She looked at me for a few seconds and hugged me strongly again, almost solemnly.

"Hey, is everything all right? It's not like you're running away like last time...! I'll be offended if you don't come today!"

"No, don't worry about it, it's just that I have a long day ahead of me, it's the last one before the Christmas vacation..."

"I understand. Perhaps we return to Bali for New Year's

Eve, what do you say?"

"Perhaps! I'll get going, I am running late. See you later Oliver!"

"Have a good day Ryn!"

She kissed me and rushed out the door. She had left me hot coffee on the table, with the last pack of chocolate cookies to go with it.

I loved her little acts of love she had towards me, they made me feel special and put me in a good mood. Yet there was something strange in her look when she left. Anyway, I tried not to think about it too much and concentrate on the final details of the presentation.

Around four o'clock I started to prepare myself. I was still undecided what I was going to wear. I opened the closet and found another surprise. There was a designer bag with a red bow, accompanied by a card:

"This is your early Christmas present! As soon as I noticed it, I immediately saw it on you. I thought that having lived the last year in flip-flops and shorts, your wardrobe was a bit unprepared for your big event!

Love, Ryn."

It contained a very elegant light blue jacket that fit me like a glove. She was fantastic, even in the tensest moments she always managed to calm me down.

After having dressed up, I finally went to the bookstore where the event took place. My publisher, represented by a stumpy, curly-haired little man with a red goatee named Carlo, perpetually with sweaty armpits, was already going crazy. There were more people than we could imagine in our wildest dreams and the chairs were not enough, so Carlo began to annoy me and the staff with his apocalyptic anxieties, squawking back and forth like a chicken.

At six o'clock, we somehow managed to start the event; there must have been at least two hundred people staring at me on that sort of poorly prepared stage, which initially awed me a bit.

Then, I recognised my friends in the crowd: Elisa and Alberto were in the front row; there were also Daniele and Gianluca, whom I hadn't seen for ages, and even Oreste, who had saved me from that wretched Christmas Eve so many years ago; and last, late as always, Ryn arrived too, accompanied by…My mother.

We exchanged a quick glance. She gave me a clumsy smile, with her eyes that seemed to ask for a second chance. I was surprised and amazed but full of joy. They were all there for me, friends old and new, sharing my moment of glory, in what turned into a great general celebration. It was one of the happiest moments ever.

My presentation lasted just over an hour and culminated with a long applause and a surprise, which I had promised Elisa and Alberto.

"Thank you all very much for coming. Before leaving, I would like to announce a piece of important news: given its recent success, our online newspaper has been officially registered, also thanks to the help of the new sponsors, who will finance the whole project, so we decided to drastically expand its contents. We are looking for journalists and web content writers to join our team; if you are interested, you can contact Alberto Grestini, the new editor of the newspaper, and Elisa Rossetti, our new web designer! A hug to everyone and Merry Christmas!"

I dragged them on stage with their shocked faces, to give them one last applause.

Once off the stage, they looked at me perplexed:

"Oliver but...What does that mean...?"

"Did you get it? I would like you, Alby, to be the new director of my newspaper. You have always been the best and I need you. Unless you would rather continue to be a butcher at your father's, but I think your talent is wasted there! And Elisa, I have followed your work over the years. You have become really good and I need your help to make the leap. Obviously, you will have a generous fixed salary, which we will discuss together. You have always been loyal friends under all circumstances and I would like to continue together. After all, I promised you that one day I would hire you in my newspaper! What do you say?"

Both of them were amazed. They looked at each other for a few seconds, still in disbelief, and they enthusiastically accepted my proposal. Somehow, we have reunited again, like the old days.

"Now I will leave you, I have an important appointment. It was nice to see you again, we'll talk soon about the details!"

"Thanks, boss! See you soon and Merry Christmas!"

We hugged each other tightly and I left, making my way through the crowd.

I looked for Ryn, but I couldn't see her anywhere. My mother was still there; and I found myself face to face with her.

"Congratulations Oliver, it was a beautiful event; and you did a great thing to help your friends, I am proud of you".

"Where's Ryn?"

"She left... She didn't tell you?"

"Told me what?"

"She's going back to Korea today. She said her work here is finished."

26.

I could not and did not want to believe her words. Why did she always have to leave like that? I tried to call her immediately, but her cell phone was turned off.

I sank into despair, putting my hands in my hair. My mother approached me, putting her hand on my shoulder.

"Her plane is in two hours' time; come on, I'll take you to the airport!"

"I don't know if I should follow her. This is the second time she has run away like this. What's more, this time without even an explanation."

"Oliver...If you really care about her, go, don't let her get away. Don't make the same mistake I did. Go get her!"

I looked up, seeing my mother's determined gaze.

"All right, let's go!"

We left the bookstore in a hurry and got into the car. It started snowing heavily, for the first time in several years, which whitened the whole city of Rome instantly, making traffic at rush hour even more unbearable than usual.

"We will never make it in time with the car. I'll leave you here near Termini station, there is a train to Fiumicino airport that leaves in four minutes; the next one is in an hour…If it turns up. Good luck Oliver!"

"...Thank you, mum...!"

I got out of the car and rushed in a race against time, risking to be almost hit by a scooter. But there was no time to think about anything else, I had to get on that train. I watched the seconds go by on the clock, three and a half minutes had already passed.

I found myself in front of the central board, where around fifty departures and arrivals were listed. It took me another twenty seconds to find the right track from which my train was leaving: track 24. Fuck it was the farthest! And only ten seconds to reach it.

With almost no breath in my body and little hope left, I threw myself into one last desperate shot. Two meters from the track, I heard the train conductor's whistle and the doors closing.

"No!! Wait, I beg you!"

He didn't care about me, giving me just a distracted look, preparing himself to climb into his position. I had not made it just for a handful of seconds.

I saw the image of Ryn fade into my mind, like a beautiful dream from which I never wanted to wake up, but which ended there.

I sat on a bench beside the train with my head down, trying to catch my breath as I waited to see that train leave and take away my last hope.

Suddenly, a rather bizarre character appeared, probably drunk and a bit crazy, laughing and shouting at the same time as rambling phrases, who stole the train conductor's whistle, staging his very personal show, while the latter was trying to chase him, swearing at him loudly. After a few minutes, he was stopped by a security officer and the doors opened again for a couple of seconds, allowing me to sneak inside. While they were taking him away, I met his eyes and smiled at him from the window, full of gratitude and he winked back at me, continuing to laugh and yell for no apparent reason. That madman had been my saviour!

Along the way, I tried to contact Ryn several times, without ever succeeding.

I arrived at the airport at half-past eight, thirty-five minutes before her departure. The airport was packed with people returning home to celebrate Christmas with their families, which made the task even harder. Also, there was a good chance that she had already checked in, but as I had got there, I had to give it a try.

Once again, I found myself in front of the departure board: there was only one flight to Korea, going to Seoul; it could only be that one. I ran back to terminal three, in the faint hope of intercepting her before losing her again.

I managed to reach it in a few minutes, amid a fleet of passengers whizzing in every direction. I looked everywhere, in all the coffee shops, stores and at the check-in counters, but there was no trace of her. I realised how utopian it was to think I could find her in the middle of that mess. Maybe it had been a stupid idea and it was right for her to get out of my life as she had entered it, on tiptoe and without disturbing me.

I took one last look around before I went outside. I thought I saw a familiar face just beyond the security area, or maybe it was just my imagination that wanted it to be her.

"RYN??" I shouted her name three times, with all the breath in my body. She turned and saw me, it was really her.

"Ryn!! Where are you going?! Why are you leaving me here like this again?!"

She stared at me with bright eyes and a smile of resignation on her face. Then, without saying anything, she waved her hand, turned around and continued to walk, until I couldn't see her anymore.

I had lost her, probably forever. I kept watching the security for a few minutes, without being able to give myself an explanation of what had just happened.

Feeling depressed, I got out of the airport. It kept snowing and I was soaking wet, but at that moment I didn't care much. I picked up the phone to try to call her one last time and noticed an email I had received just one hour earlier.

"Dear Oliver,

I wanted to congratulate you on your presentation today, it was a great success!

I didn't have the courage to tell you this morning, but I decided to go back to Korea.

I am really happy that you found your mother again. I talked a lot with her today and you have no idea what she went through. Try giving her a second chance. I know very well what kind of environment the Kaiwon is, how shady it is and how it can affect a person's life. Precisely for this reason, I believe that our lives travel on two totally different tracks and it would not be right to involve you again in a situation that already took away the person dearest to you, you do not deserve it.

I think I have fallen in love with you and only now do I fully understand that loving, sometimes, implies letting go. With deep sadness in my heart as I write these words, I think it is time to say goodbye. I hope one day you can forgive me for this, it is the best decision for both of us.

I will always be grateful to have met you and I will always remember you with love.

Good luck my dear Oliver, I wish you all the best.

Love, Ryn."

I sat on the bench in despair, letting the snowflakes mix with my tears, thinking how tremendously unfair it all was.

I was trying to convince myself that, in the end, maybe it really was the best solution; after all, we come from two totally different worlds and everyone had to go their own way, as she had said. But the more I repeated it to myself, the less I believed it. And the thought of never meeting her again made me sadder and sadder, I couldn't give myself peace, crying like a child, squatting on that bench.

After about twenty minutes, I began to feel the cold penetrating through my soaked clothes and I began to think that I had to make up for it: Ryn would never come back.

I took one last look at the airport, lifting my eyes to the sky, just in time to notice her plane taking off. It was really over. I closed my eyes for a few seconds and decided to go home.

But just when I was about to get up, my wet and cold body was wrapped in a warm and intense familiar embrace, with that unmistakable scent of powdered sugar.

I looked up and saw Ryn's smiling face, lined with tears, leaning on my shoulder. My heart burst with joy. Only she was capable of taking me from hell to heaven in a few moments. I turned towards her and held her tightly to me, taking her face in my hands and kissing her like I had never kissed her before.

"Forgive me Oliver, I apologise deeply! I was a fool to leave like that. I am sorry, I am so sorry!"

"Stop apologising now, I have never been happier to see you! Rather tell me... Why didn't you leave?"

"I thought about what was the right thing to do. And then the one that would have made me happy. And for the first time in my life, I chose the second. I decided that I no longer want to be without you. If it's all right with you, of course!"

"It's all right with me...If you stop running away!"

"I will never run away again, I promise you!"

I held her tightly to me, stroking her hair, still in disbelief that she was in my arms again. All my anxieties, disappointments and bad thoughts, vanished in that magical and wonderful moment, leaving room only for an infinite joy.

At that moment, a car not far away honked and rolled down the window.

"Do you need a ride?!"

A brief gasp and an exchange of glances, in which there was everything we had never said to each other. There was my mother, moved and smiling, beaming with happiness.

We went to her apartment, all three of us together, stopping for a few days to celebrate the holidays. How beautiful it was to sit on that couch, embraced by my dearest women, with the soft light, the illuminated Christmas tree and that ancient scent of freshly baked cookies. I felt really good there with them, like I had never felt before. I was finally in the right place at the right time and wanted nothing more.

Christmas many years ago had taken my father and almost all my hopes away from me; this one, instead, had given me back my mother and the only girl I had ever really loved.

Without a doubt, a beautiful Christmas gift. The best one there is, in the most beautiful place in the world.

Right where I belong.

Somewhere I Belong by Davide R. Battaglia,

ISBN: 978-0-578-79301-6. *© 2021*

Acknowledgements

Thanks to my mother and father, my most solid and essential certainties, who gave me the freedom to build my life in my own way, constantly supporting me, even morally, at any time, cushioning my falls, always offering a word of comfort, giving me, in their own way, love and understanding and teaching me that there is always an alternative way.

Thanks to my brothers, Emanuele and Marco, tough men, brilliant at times, distant but quietly present, whom I know I can always count on.

Thanks to my grandmother, always my first fan, who never stopped believing in me, even when I was not right or when, as she would say, you could not see the sun at the end of the storm, nor the sunrise at the end of a very long night; and to my grandfather, who taught me humility and benevolence, always with simplicity.

Thanks to Uncle Roberto and Aunt Luisa, steady pillars of my life, always ready to give me a smile.

Thanks to Sonia, Luca, Tim, Emanuele C., Fabio, Liza, Valerio and Fabrizio, the "Londoner" friends of a lifetime and companions of a thousand (dis)adventures, who've helped me to survive.

Thanks to my friend Valentina, my safe haven for over twenty years, to whom it is always nice to return back.

Thanks to Sarah, Jill and Darren, real superstars, who made this possible.

Thanks to Minjung, a source of daily inspiration, without which I would not have made it.

Thanks to all those people I met along the way, who welcomed me and helped me with what they had, even if only with a good word.

Thanks to YOU who are reading, for giving me a chance and reading my first book.

To all of you, THANK YOU from the bottom of my heart!

I hope you enjoyed reading my first novel. If it gave you some food for thought, kept you company or just helped experience some enjoyable moments and you are curious to find out more, please visit my official Instagram account to see the settings and places

described in the book!

Thank you, and stay tuned!

Printed in Great Britain
by Amazon